"You want me to confess I'm everything you think I am."

Lineesa added, "And if I'm not, are you afraid you'll not be able to hate me as much as you'd like to?"

"Perhaps," David responded coolly, "but I think that's happened already, you see. I find that words like hate and revenge don't spring to mind so easily when I think of you these days. I really want to get to the bottom of you, Lin, because in some ways you've proved me wrong. So I'm offering a truce."

Lineesa was stunned. "Wouldn't it be simpler just to let me go?"

"Maybe," he conceded. "But then I could be spending the rest of my life wondering about you—and concerned. And you. . . . Well, let's just say this is a better way."

Was David's truce a test? Or was it a trap?

LINDSAY ARMSTRONG was working for Lufthansa Airlines when she met and married an accountant from New Zealand. They decided to settle—if you can call it that—in Australia. Early on they blithely embarked on an epic camping trip, which carried them from coast to coast with their four children. Then they moved on to a six-hundred-acre mixed grain property, which they eventually abandoned to the mice, the leeches and the constant black flies. Undaunted, they purchased an untried trotter—"mainly because he had blue eyes"—and went on to win twenty-seven purses. Now they've opted for a more conventional life in Brisbane, where Lindsay started writing and continued raising their five children. But when Lindsay looks to the future, she doesn't imagine for one moment they will stay put forever.

Books by Lindsay Armstrong

HARLEQUIN PRESENTS
607—ENTER MY JUNGLE
806—SAVED FROM SIN
871—FINDING OUT

HARLEQUIN ROMANCE
2497—MY DEAR INNOCENT
2582—PERHAPS LOVE
2653—DON'T CALL IT LOVE

These books may be available at your local bookseller.

Don't miss any of our special offers. Write to us at the following address for information on our newest releases.

Harlequin Reader Service
901 Fuhrmann Blvd.
P.O. Box 1325, Buffalo, NY 14269
Canadian address: P.O. Box 2800, Postal Station A,
5170 Yonge St., Willowdale, Ont. M2N 6J3

LINDSAY ARMSTRONG

finding out

Harlequin Books

TORONTO • NEW YORK • LONDON
AMSTERDAM • PARIS • SYDNEY • HAMBURG
STOCKHOLM • ATHENS • TOKYO • MILAN

Harlequin Presents first edition April 1986
ISBN 0-373-10871-0

Original hardcover edition published in 1985
by Mills & Boon Limited

CHAPTER ONE

LINEESA Marchmont stretched and yawned and viewed the sunlight pouring through her bedroom window with narrowed eyes. There was something about this bright new shining day that was faintly menacing. But she couldn't immediately recall what lay on her soul like a dark cloud that was quite contrary in spirit to the sunlight that lay in a bar across the end of her bed.

Then it hit her like the kick of a rifle. It was her wedding anniversary, her first wedding anniversary.

'Oh *hell*,' she muttered and twisted restlessly in the wide bed.

The bedroom was large and beautifully decorated with apricot wallpaper, voluminous ivory Thai-silk drapes, a close-pile apricot carpet that felt like velvet, some magnificent pieces of very old cedar furniture with brass fittings and two pale, sherbet-green upholstered arm-chairs set in front of a fireplace. It was in fact the master bedroom at Marchmont where apricot had been someone's favourite colour for the outside walls of the two-storied house were a soft, mellow, apricot stucco, the colour you find on gum trees when they've shed their bark; and all the windows were framed by green, louvered shutters, the colour of gum leaves. But it was an effective colour scheme for a house set largely in a bush setting—it blended well, Lineesa often thought.

She pushed aside the bedclothes reluctantly but

didn't get up straight away. It was as if the act of getting up would set the seal of inevitability on this day. Then she chided herself for being fanciful and slid off the bed. Whatever she did, there was no getting away from this day, just as there had been no getting away from the three hundred and sixty four days that had preceeded it. And anyway, what difference would this day make?

But as she stood in a pool of sunlight that revealed the slenderness of her waist and the full, rounded curves of her breasts and hips and her long, lovely legs through her sheer nightgown, she felt her nerves tighten at the thought of what lay ahead, and she knew it was going to be a harder day to survive than most. And she clenched her fists unconsciously, then realised it and forced herself to take a deep steadying breath, and walk through to the adjoining bathroom.

The bathroom that adjoined the master bedroom at Marchmont had fascinated her when she'd first seen it. The walls and floor were lined with champagne-gold Italian marble as was the sunken bath that was the size of a small swimming pool and could be activated to be a spa. A crystal chandelier hung above the bath and real jade jars and powder bowls stood on the marble vanity unit. And there were always jade-green towels, facecloths and even jade-green soap in this bathroom.

But as she usually did in the mornings, Lineesa by-passed the sybaritic pleasures of the sunken bath in favour of a brisk shower.

She dressed casually in jeans and a T-shirt and spent about five minutes brushing her long hair that was mid-way between fair and light brown. It was strong, vital hair and apart from getting it trimmed regularly, she didn't have to do much else to it because it had the body to lie loose in a golden cloud to below her shoulders, or to be put up.

This morning she tied it back with an aquamarine scarf that matched her T-shirt, and sat down to do her face. It was a face that a lot of people recognised because Lineesa had been a highly successful photographic model before her marriage and had been seen frequently on the pages of glossy magazines and on television commercials, and like many faces seen thus, it was striking. But her most successful, memorable assignment had been modelling a car, a luxury limousine, and the series of advertisements had featured her partly underneath it in a mechanic's boilersuit with a smudge of grease on her cheek; in a chauffeur's uniform with cap holding the door open for her companion; in a strikingly feminine version of a man's pin-striped suit with a high collar and tie, sitting behind the wheel with her companion beside her, and finally, in a gorgeous but rather revealing evening dress and a silver mink stole, this time in the back seat and again with companion.

Her companion had been almost as successful as she had—an enormous, shaggy, old-English sheep dog. And the slogan that had accompanied the advertisement had said simply . . . *Get the car first, the girls will follow—the dog we leave up to you.*

But she'd had no inkling at the time how she was going to live to bitterly regret the slogan and the ad.

She thought of it now as she sat before the mirror and applied a light moisturiser to her smooth golden skin. The dog had at first refused point blank to set foot in the car. Then it had had a change of heart and taken such a liking to it only the largest juiciest bone had enticed it out. It had also taken a great liking to Lineesa and over the three days of the assignment this liking had turned to a deep love so that whenever it spotted her it would jump up and lick her face enthusiastically, and whenever they were in the car together it would try to sit on her lap, thereby nearly smothering her . . .

But who could have foreseen it was to have such a tragic outcome? she thought as she had so many times before. *If* . . . But she deliberately cut her thoughts off at that point and stared instead at her face in the mirror. It was eighteen months since the car ads had come out, eighteen long months, surely there must be some visible changes in that face? Yet she could detect none. The hazel eyes beneath strongly marked eyebrows were still the same, the slightly square jaw, which someone had once said gave her face an intriguing quality and rescued it from being just pretty, was still the same, and the cool elegant lips which someone else had once said, drove him mad . . . it was all still the same.

'And what do you expect?' she murmured. 'Faces don't change, it's your soul that changes, grows to feel old and . . . bitter.' She shut her eyes and gritted her teeth, and jumped as someone knocked on the door.

'It's only me, ma'am,' Mrs Livingstone, the housekeeper, said as she poked her head round the door. 'Mr Smith is here and he would like to check the last details of the party with you.'

Lineesa grimaced and glanced at her watch. 'He's about bright and early. All right, ask him if he'd like to have breakfast with me. I'll be down in a minute.'

* * *

'Well, Mr Smith,' she said as she entered the breakfast room, 'do sit down. What would you like?' she asked as she crossed to the sideboard. 'Bacon and eggs or . . . grilled fish?'

'I've already had breakfast, thank-you, Mrs Marchmont,' the tall, bespectacled young man said just a little awkwardly.

Lineesa glanced at him through her lashes, sensing something about him that wasn't quite in keeping with the efficient, business-like air he normally wore so well that she'd assumed he was the perfect personal assistant cum private secretary right through to his soul. 'What is it?' she said, and frowned faintly as he jerked his eyes away from hers. 'Has something terrible happened? Have the caterers gone out of business unexpectedly or . . .?'

'Oh no!' He looked back at her, now so patently horrified that she had to grin. But he didn't return her grin. Instead he cleared his throat and swallowed visibly and with a gesture of futility that was strangely touching, turned away from her to stare out of the windows that overlooked the terrace and the long, sloping lawn that led down to the shimmering waters of the river. Then he appeared to take a grip on himself and he turned back and said quietly, 'No, nothing's wrong at all.'

'Good. You had me worried for a moment,' Lineesa murmured, but remained unconvinced. She dished herself up a fillet of grilled fish and sat down. 'At least have a cup of coffee,' she added.

He complied and looked at her enquiringly. 'May I pour you one too?'

'Thank-you. Mmmm . . . that was delicious,' she said a few minutes later and pushed her plate away. 'I suspect Mr Livingstone was up very early this morning to catch that. All right,' she wiped her mouth delicately with the linen napkin and reached for her coffee cup, 'let's get down to work. By the way, seeing as we've known each other for almost twelve months to the day,' there was a slight tinge of irony in her voice, 'do I have to keep calling you Mr Smith?'

'Not at all, Mrs Marchmont,' Michael Smith said evenly so that Lineesa concluded that whatever had been bothering him earlier was no longer a problem. 'My name is Michael. Please use whichever you prefer.'

Lineesa studied him obliquely, still slightly puzzled. She guessed he was about twenty-four, three years older than she was but he had a sort of boyish look about him that made him seem younger—until one encountered his business-like gravity and his undoubted acumen at organising things. And then one realised that the boyish impression came only from the fact that he was very tall and thin and sometimes had difficulty in disposing of his arms and legs and never more so than in a car.

'Very well, Michael,' she observed with a faint shrug. 'I don't suppose there's any chance of you returning the compliment?'

'No, ma'am,' he replied and for the first time that morning, permitted himself a small smile. 'Uh . . .' he added hastily, and delved into his briefcase, 'I have the final figures here. There'll be twenty people altogether for dinner, of whom six will be staying the night.' He named the six, two married couples and two other people. 'And there will be seventy-six people at the ball . . .' His voice trailed off and he stared at Lineesa who had made an abrupt movement with her hand and knocked over the salt cellar. 'Is something wrong?' he said at last. 'You look . . . as if you've seen a ghost . . .'

Lineesa raised her eyes to his and he flinched visibly at the scorching look of anger and scorn he saw in their hazel depths. And something else he couldn't name.

'No,' she said with an effort. 'No, nothing's wrong.' She strove to speak precisely and unhurriedly. 'It's just,' she stood up suddenly, 'that I think Mrs Livingstone can deal with all this as well as I can. Would you . . . would ring for her? I'm sorry but,' she swallowed, 'I think I'll go for a ride before it gets too hot. Yes, that's what I'll do. Please excuse me . . .' She turned away and stumbled towards the door.

'Mrs Marchmont!' Michael Smith's voice was anxious and urgent.

Lineesa turned back. 'It will be all right,' she said vaguely. 'Mrs Livingstone was doing this long before I came . . .'

'I . . . I guess so. Er . . . Mr Marchmont asked me to tell you that he might be a little late but not to worry, he'll be here . . .'

'Oh, I don't doubt that,' Lineesa said through her teeth and left the room.

The sun was hot on her back as she lay face down in the warm, sweet-smelling grass. And the only sounds she could hear were the warbling of some magpies in the trees and her horse cropping the grass contentedly.

She wasn't sure how long she'd lain like that but she'd ridden for a good hour as if pursued by all the demons in hell, and then taken pity on the horse and jumped down and flung herself on to the grass after removing its bridle, half-hoping in a curiously demented way that it would gallop off and leave her. But it had only started to graze, never moving far from her prone, rigid body.

She turned over and was surprised to see that the sun was almost overhead, and with a sigh she sat up and rubbed her face wearily. Then she moved a few feet so that she could lean back against a tree trunk and she pulled a long stalk of grass and started to chew it, and to think coherently for the first time since Michael Smith had mentioned that name—Catherine Corbett.

'That's what did it,' she muttered to herself. 'That's what made me so mad I couldn't think straight ... that's what made me feel like strangling someone. I never imagined he was living like a monk but Cathy Corbett! Is it all part of the plan? If it's not ... but it has to be because two people have now alluded to her and him in my hearing and for my benefit, and one so-called friend has whispered in my ear—watch out for Cathy. And now she'd be spending the night at Marchmont, and tomorrow she'll be part of the picnic that's planned ... Oh yes, it has to be part of the plan, the humiliation, but I won't stand for this! Enough is ... Dear God, how long do I have to go on paying for something I *didn't* do! Or did I ...?'

She closed her eyes and leant her head back against the tree trunk. And immediately an image of Piers Marchmont rose in her mind. Piers with his young, thin face and laughing blue eyes, Piers who had driven into her life one day in the same model car as had been used in the advertisement, with the same kind of dog sitting in the front seat, and who'd introduced himself gravely, and said with his eyes dancing, 'I got the car, I thought you looked as if you rather liked the dog, so I got one of him too. All I need now is ... you.'

Lineesa had stared and then burst out laughing. 'But how did you find me?' she'd demanded finally.

He'd waved a negligent hand at the block of flats she'd just come out of and said, 'I got your address from a secret source, a mate of mine to be precise. He . . . er . . . dates your flatmate. And when I happened to mention how taken I was with you, your pictures at least, he told me smugly that he knew you. The rest was easy. Do you mind?' he'd added seriously.

'I . . . you didn't *buy* the car . . .'

'Yes I did. But don't worry, I needed a new car. I . . . er . . . stole the dog. That, if nothing else, must prove to you how genuine I am. Will you have dinner with me on the strength of it?'

Lineesa had blinked and been unable to stop the smile that had trembled on her lips. 'Are you recommending yourself as a genuine dog-napper? Because if so . . .'

'Well, actually I borrowed him. He belongs to my sister. Do you know she's going into breeding them now? And all thanks to you, did you know *that*?' His blue eyes had teased her a little.

'Yes,' she'd said wryly. 'I'm told they've suddenly become much in demand as a breed—more so than the car! But there's an old saying, isn't there? Never share the spotlight with animals or children, they tend to steal it.'

'Ah,' Piers Marchmont had said wisely, 'that's not true in this case. The truth is that the breed has become popular because the dog was the only thing in the ad most people could acquire quite easily. And in acquiring it, they could dream a little—by association. The men of having a marvellous looking girl like you to . . . have and to hold, and the women of becoming a marvellous looking girl like you!'

'That sounds like reverse psychology if ever I heard it,' Lineesa had murmured. And added a shade ruefully, 'Where does the car stand? That's what it was supposed to be all about.'

'*Voilà,*' he'd said and gestured towards the car with a flourish. 'You perceive one very satisfied customer for the car too. But seriously, will you have dinner with me?'

She'd succumbed and that's where it had all started.

'Or did it?' Lineesa asked herself as a dappled shaft of sunlight fell on her face so that she opened her eyes and squinted and shut them again to see a kaleidoscope of shooting colours behind her lids.

Perhaps the roots of it went even deeper, she reflected and grasped another blade of grass. Right back in fact to the day my father died when I was two, leaving my mother to fend for herself—a thing she wasn't very good at . . .

A vision of her childhood threaded its way through Lineesa's mind. Her mother came from a gentile, upper middle-class English background, which had left her quite unprepared for the harsh reality of bringing up a child single-handedly in a faraway country that she didn't even particularly like. Not that she'd ever admitted it, because the one thing she'd made a stand about in her life, had been her devotion to the young, fair-haired Royal Australian Air Force mechanic who'd met her on a tour of the British Isles, swept her off her feet and to the horror of her parents, taken her away to the Antipodes to live. But only three years later, the young blonde mechanic had been killed in an air crash and Lineesa's mother had been left with a baby daughter, no in-laws, and a devotion to a memory that was to cost her dear. She'd fallen out with her own parents over the marriage and the death of her husband had intensified her sense of hurt at her parents' attitude that she'd married beneath herself. So a reconciliation had never been made, and she'd struggled on trying to make a life for herself and Lineesa, ekeing out her pension by taking in laundry and sewing, yet curiously, trying to instil into her daughter that very sense of gentility she'd so resented when applied to herself, and had found such a handicap in that it had fitted her for nothing once the only man by whom she'd been taken, was gone.

The result of this up-bringing had been almost as curious as the circumstances that had led to it. Lineesa had grown up with one burning ambition ... to make money. Enough money to set her mother up in a comfortable little house of her own with all the small pleasures in life that she'd forgone for so long. But it had been that ambition that had brought her into conflict with her mother ...

During her senior year at high-school, Lineesa had fought a battle with her mother and her school teachers. Her teachers had wanted her to go on to university. Her mother, when apprised of this, had taken a quivering breath and said, yes. Yes!

But Lineesa had looked around the cramped, cheap little Housing Commission flat they occupied in a high-rise mausoleum of a building that couldn't have been more different from the minor English manor house where her mother had grown up, and often told Lineesa about, and said stubbornly, no.

And it was only to her history teacher that she had confessed the reason behind her stubbornness.

'I want to support my mother for a change. I know—I know, I could apply for all sorts of grants and the tuition's free but it will still mean she'll have to go on washing and ironing for other people. No, I'm going to make some money!'

'How?' her teacher had enquired sadly. 'Have you thought of that?'

'Not yet, but I will.'

'Lineesa, you have a fine brain ... Are you going to throw it away to become some dim little check-out girl? And how much money do you think you're going to make at that?'

'I don't think you can throw your brain away,' she'd answered with a grin. 'But no, I'm going to make more than that.'

Yet when the opportunity to do this had presented itself, she hadn't recognised it at first. She'd starred in the school play in her last term, and a picture of the principals had appeared in a newspaper. Two days later, a strange woman had come up to her as she left the school grounds, and looked at her pigtails with a funny little smile on her face, then offered her a card which bore the name of a modelling agency, and asked her if she'd ever considered photographic modelling as a career.

'You're joking!' Lineesa had said blankly.

'Oh no,' the woman had replied and held up the picture from the paper. 'You have the most photogenic features I've seen for a long time. However, it is a cut-throat, competitive, sometimes ultra-bitchy kind of business to be in but if you reach the top you make a lot of money—and I think you have the face to reach the top. If you're interested, come and see me sometime.'

Lineesa had had the sense to get the school guidance officer to check the agency out, and his report had been good—it seemed it was a genuine modelling agency of some repute, he'd said, but had added the rider that anyone thinking of entering the world of modelling should think twice . . .

She'd thought it out a hundred times. Then, the day after school had broken up, for the last time for her, she'd gone into town with the card, and come home several hours later to present her mother with a *fait accompli*.

But her mother had been horrified and begged her not to do it. 'Why not take a secretarial course if you don't want to go to University, or *something* . . . we can scrape together the money for that. But not this!' she'd pleaded tearfully.

'Why not?' Lineesa had shot at her.

'Because . . . well, it's not quite lady-like! Well-brought up girls don't . . .'

'This one does,' Lineesa had said grimly. 'And anyway you're being a bit old-fashioned, Mummy dear. That might have been the case when you were a girl but these days I don't think it follows automatically that all models are scarlet fallen women if *that's* what you mean. Besides which, if people can't judge me for myself, then they needn't bother . . .

How ironic, Lineesa thought, coming back to the present. How supremely ironic that I should have said that. Because that's exactly how I was judged only it was worse. I was judged as hard and mercenary, and a tart. But not by Piers. No, Piers fell in love with me, or thought he did. But because he was different, and because he was such a clown, I didn't really know what he was feeling . . . until it was too late.

A solitary tear slid down her cheek and she licked the saltiness of it from her top lip and thought about Piers Marchmont—a thing she prevented herself from doing whenever possible because of the pain it caused her. But today seemed to be a day for hurting herself, she reflected . . .

She'd been modelling for three years when Piers had driven into her life. Three years during which she'd discovered that everything everyone had told her about the business had been true. It *was* a cut-throat, bitchy, heart-breaking business. But the thing she'd never admitted to anyone, was that her mother, her unworldly, old-fashioned mother, had been as right as anyone about it.

Summed up, Lineesa had thought to herself bitterly one day, the fact is that when your face and body are your stock in trade, there *is* something not quite nice about it. Men approach you with but one thought in mind, and other women tend to steer clear of you . . .

At first, it had been a little heady to see the admiration in most men's eyes when they'd looked at her, and because she'd been very young it had been hard not to let it go to her head. But some frankly unpleasant experiences had cured her of that and left in its place a wariness and a cynicism. They don't want me, she'd told herself once, they only want my body.

But despite it all, she'd pressed on and the other prediction about the business had come true too. She'd saved enough money to put a deposit on a house for her mother, and counted it all worth while to see her mother's touching, childish delight when she'd moved in and when she'd been made welcome in the seaside area, invited to join the local bridge club and a theatre group and so on. Not that her mother had ever quite come to terms with Lineesa's profession. In fact she was always at pains to tell her new found friends that her daughter was only *temporarily* in the business, as if that removed the stigma of having a model for a daughter. But Lineesa had known that if any breath of scandal ever attached itself to her name, her mother would die a little and probably never be able to face her friends again.

But when Piers Marchmont had entered Lineesa's life, he'd somehow contrived to slip under her guard. She'd had dinner with him that first night and on the way home said to him with a rather brutal sort of candour, 'If you're wondering how to broach the subject of us going to bed, maybe I can save you the trouble. I don't sleep around . . . Perhaps I should have mentioned that before you paid for my dinner.'

His hands had tightened on the wheel as if he was angry and she'd turned her head away and sighed. But he'd surprised her. He'd said after a moment, 'You shouldn't judge all leopards by their spots, Lineesa . . .'

'It's hard not to . . .' Somehow, without her quite knowing how or why, her voice had betrayed her and a world of hurt had been conveyed in those few words.

'I'm sorry,' he'd said at last. 'Will you . . . could you just promise me one thing? If you let me see you again, will you . . . let me speak for myself . . .?'

She hadn't answered yes or no. But she'd seen him again and they'd drifted into a kind of relationship she'd no longer believed existed. They'd become firm friends. And because he was a Marchmont, albeit the second son, they had attracted some publicity when they were seen at parties and so on, together, and a certain amount of speculation in the circles in which they moved.

Neither the publicity nor the speculation had escaped Lineesa's mother.

'No, Mum,' Lineesa had said to her one day, 'I haven't met the rest of the family. You see I'm not *going* with him precisely. We're friends, that's all.'

'His parents are dead, you know,' her mother had said knowledgeably. 'His older brother is now the head of the family. His name is David, and I believe he has a sister.'

'Yes he does,' Lineesa had smiled faintly. 'She breeds old-English sheep dogs.'

'Then you know her?'

'No. I know her dog . . .'

'Lineesa,' her mother had said in exasperation, 'how can that be?'

Lineesa had sighed inwardly. 'Mum . . .'

But her mother had gone back to her musings. 'I don't know how far the family goes back but they have to be very wealthy. They're into shipping I believe and a host of . . .'

'Piers claims some of his ancestors were highwaymen and others remittance men. He says they have a skeleton lurking in every cupboard.'

Her mother had looked faintly worried but her brow had cleared almost immediately. 'Oh well, most families do. He was probably teasing you anyway. I do know his brother David went to Oxford and was a rowing blue, did you know that?'

'I don't know anything at all about David Marchmont, nor do I want to,' Lineesa had yawned. 'But as a matter of interest, how do you know so much about them?'

'I read all about them in the *Woman's Weekly*,' her mother had said primly. 'There was this article a couple of years ago. They have this fantastic house which is *called* Marchmont at . . .' she wrinkled her brow again, 'Wiseman's Ferry, that's it! It's on the Hawkesbury. That's only—roughly

thirty miles from Sydney—but perhaps you've
been there?'

Lineesa had shaken her head.

'Doesn't Piers live there?

'Well, he has a flat at Rose Bay . . .'

'Hasn't he even told you about Marchmont?'

'No. Mum, Piers and I are just friends!' She'd
smiled at her mother lovingly. 'So don't go getting
your hopes up for the society wedding of the year
for your only daughter . . .'

But in her heart of hearts, Lineesa had wondered
about that, her claim that she and Piers were only
friends. True, Piers had very rarely tried to over-
step the boundaries of friendship and when he
had, it had always been with a teasing little smile
but just sometimes she'd detected something more
in his eyes. And she'd thought, I'm being naïve to
think this is not leading up to something. And she
had sometimes wondered what she'd do if that
something was brought out into the open. At least
she liked Piers, liked him a lot. Enough to want to
live with him though? Or sleep with him to be
precise . . .

But I don't seem to think of him like that, she'd
reflected once.

And in almost the same breath she'd had to
admit that no man seemed to fit into that context
any longer. The days of feeling her pulse-beat
accelerate over an attractive man appeared to have
passed with a lot of her naïvety. Is that crazy when
you're only twenty? she'd asked herself. But her
answering thought had been that she felt a lot older
than twenty—except when she was with Piers
Marchmont. Then she felt about fifteen and
sometimes she found herself wishing fervently she
was only fifteen.

And with a chance to take another road.

So she'd drifted on for several months, seeing a lot of Piers Marchmont, falling in with a lot of his madcap ideas—like the day he'd taken her to the races and introduced her to all his numerous acquaintances as a cousin of the Queen . . .

'*Piers!*' she'd whispered out of the corner of her mouth after the first introduction which had taken her as much by surprise as it had the portly, middle-aged gentleman on the receiving end of it, although he'd doffed his hat and bowed low over her hand. 'Have you gone mad?'

'Not at all. You *look* the part. Lovely and regal and blue-blooded. I mean that in the figurative sense of the phrase of course . . .'

'Will you shut up and listen!' she'd hissed at him. 'Too many people know my face. And anyway as soon as I open my mouth they'll realise . . .'

'Don't open it then,' he'd said serenely. 'Just smile and look gracious. But we can always tell them you've lived in Australia long enough to acquire the accent.'

'Piers . . .'

But nothing she'd said had daunted him in the slightest. And some of the reactions to his outrageous claim had been hilarious.

So much so that once in the safety of his car at the end of the day, they'd laughed together like a couple of naughty children. Until she'd said finally, 'You do realise you've ruined me for ever, don't you? If I run into any of those people again they could have me arrested for false pretences!'

'Tell the magistrate it was April the First, which it is, had you forgotten?'

'Yes,' she'd said ruefully. 'Oh well, in that case, it was worth it I guess. But you are quite mad all the same . . . Do you have to drive so fast?'

'And it's quite beautiful to see you laugh like that, Lin,' he'd said soberly. 'Because you're the most beautiful thing I've ever seen. This is not fast, by the way.'

'No I'm not,' she'd answered automatically. But something inside her had moved warily and that feeling of wariness had remained even when he'd made no attempt to press his point. 'And it is . . . fast,' she'd murmured.

Then a curious thing had happened. Rather two curious things on the same night. Piers had taken her to a private dinner dance at an exclusive harbourside mansion. She'd worn a long clinging gown of yellow crêpe with a strapless bodice and a yellow flower in her hair, and immediately realised that this was high society—these were the true blue-bloods of Australian, at least Sydney society, she was moving in. Not that it had bothered her particularly except for the odd thought that maybe Piers was using the occasion to present her formally to his kind of people . . .

But she'd banished that thought resolutely with another one . . . it's not as if he wants to *marry* me even if he does want to sleep with me and has only been going about it in a roundabout kind of way. So he could hardly be presenting me—I'm imagining things! And she'd set out to enjoy herself.

Yet for all its exclusiveness, the party had been an awful crush which might have accounted for the fact that once, when she'd become temporarily separated from Piers, she'd looked up, straight into the eyes of a man she hadn't seen before although it was getting on for midnight.

But the silly thing had been, that she hadn't immediately looked away although the nature of what she'd seen in this strange man's eyes had been all too familiar to her. An assessing look that had stripped her naked and come back to rest on her face with a derisive gleam in a pair of cynical blue eyes.

That's when she should have looked away coolly, she'd known. Or possibly looked him up and down assessingly too and smiled derisively back. But she hadn't done either. She'd just stood there with her glass in her hand, accepting his scrutiny and feeling scorched and crazily pinned beneath it. He'd been negligently leaning against a wall when their glances had crossed, looking bored and arrogant. Then he'd straightened up, without taking his eyes off her, and she'd seen that he was tall, probably in his late thirties, fair-haired and undeniably attractive in a cold kind of way. His mouth was firm and a little cruel-looking, as if he was a man who knew what he wanted and always got it. The kind of man she least knew how to deal with—the thought had flashed across her mind. The kind of man who would only want one thing from her . . .

She'd shivered inwardly, conscious of a strange confusion. Because while she'd instantly been able to recognise these qualities in this stranger who'd looked at her so insolently, she'd not instantly been able to account for the sudden quivering of her nerves his look had aroused, the sudden, primitive awareness of her body, the clamouring of her pulses and the curious feeling at the pit of her stomach. Nor had she had any doubt that he'd been able to read all this as accurately as she'd read him.

And she'd flushed faintly and turned away a little clumsily and several minutes later had been more than normally demonstrative when Piers with his young face, laughing eyes and teasing smile had reappeared at her side. And she'd turned back defiantly but the man had gone.

Then, not half an hour later, she'd found herself sitting next to Cathy Corbett at a small table for four set on the terrace, while Piers and Cathy's escort went to procure supper for them. Cathy Corbett was the kind of girl who'd been to the right school and so on, and tended not to let one forget it, and who talked about her involvement with modelling as her 'hobby'. She was remarkably competitive about this hobby, however, and her black hair and dark eyes were quite stunning but she had a facility for looking wooden—at least that's what one photographer had said of her in Lineesa's hearing. She'd also been on the short list for the car ad, a thing that Lineesa suspected riled Cathy somewhat—that Lineesa should have won it. Then too, Cathy and Piers had been childhood friends and she often adopted a proprietorial attitude towards Piers. But only because they've known each other for so long? Lineesa had wondered once with a faint frown.

'Well, well, Lin!' Cathy had said. 'You're coming up in the world!'

'What do you mean?'

'Piers naturally! What else? He's obviously infatuated with you. Mind you,' she'd hesitated delicately, 'his family might not be. He might only be a second son but, w-e-l-l,' she'd drawled, 'I should imagine he has enough money in his own right for them to be anxious that he doesn't get trapped by someone who's more interested in his money than him.' She'd shrugged meaningfully.

You *bitch*, Lineesa had thought but not said. In fact she'd taken her time about replying and finally said unhurriedly, 'His family needn't worry on my account, Cathy.'

'Oh? Why not?'

Cathy Corbett had looked at her so guilelessly, Lineesa had lost her temper inwardly then. 'Because,' she'd said quite gently and with no real idea of what she was going to say, 'I'm after much bigger fish than Piers Marchmont. Second sons are only a . . . well, in the nature of passing the time for me. But tell me, are you really concerned for Piers or, by any chance, just plain jealous?'

Cathy Corbett had coloured richly and started to splutter incomprehensibly and Lineesa had closed her eyes disgustedly—disgusted with herself too, now that the quick burn of her anger had faded. Why had she said that? she'd wondered. About second sons . . . Apart from being untrue, it was the kind of nasty, cheap remark that had had little to distinguish it from Cathy's own brand of bitchiness.

She'd opened her eyes a moment later, only to find that over Cathy's head, she was looking for the second time that night, into a pair of cynical blue eyes set in an arrogant face but this time those eyes were filled with a look of supreme, cold disgust, before the tall, fair man, who'd eyed her earlier as if she'd been some sort of merchandise on an auction block, had turned away and disappeared indoors.

Lineesa had blinked and wondered how long he'd been there. Obviously long enough to hear her last remarks. Then Piers had arrived with two loaded plates and he'd been saying something about wanting her to meet someone, a late arrival but she'd stood up abruptly, interrupting him and pleaded a fierce headache and asked him to take her home, uncaring of Cathy Corbett's ill-concealed sneer.

But two days later, looking curiously distraught

and pale, Piers had picked her up to take her to dinner yet as soon as she'd been settled in the car, he'd said huskily, 'Lin, let's not beat about the bush anymore. Will you marry me?'

Shock had transfixed her for a long moment. Then that insidious thought had surfaced again—I didn't expect this, but would it be so bad to be married to Piers Marchmont? I *like* him more than anyone I know ... But cold sanity had returned swiftly ... I don't love him like that, though. How could I do that to him?

But it had been the hardest thing she'd ever done, to say no to him and at the same time try to convey the kind of esteem she held him in.

And in the end something in his eyes and his taut young face had hurt her so much, she'd stopped trying to explain and said unhappily, 'I'm so sorry—I just wouldn't be the right person for you. You deserve more, so much more ...' And she'd slid out of the car and fled upstairs and heard it roar away ...

Lineesa came out of her reminiscences and wiped the cold sweat off her face. The sun was still as hot as ever and the magpies were still warbling but it was always the same when she thought of Piers Marchmont.

Because the very night she'd said no to him, Piers had crashed his car at a hundred miles an hour and been killed instantly.

But if that wasn't bad enough, she'd learnt of it the next morning early and had the blame for it placed squarely at her feet ...

She swallowed hard and jumped as something warm and wet touched her arm. But it was only her horse nuzzling her gently and she turned to it gratefully, grateful to have something to take her mind elsewhere.

She stroked the soft nose. 'Are you trying to tell me we should be getting home?' she murmured. 'I guess you're right.' She glanced at her watch and her eyes widened. 'Definitely right,' she said wryly and sighed because home was not much different than thinking about Piers. All the same . . .

She slipped the bridle on and mounted easily. But they'd not gone more than a couple of miles when she felt the horse stumble and when she got down, she found it had cast a shoe and gone a little lame in the process.

She swore beneath her breath but knew there was no alternative. For one thing, Mr Livingstone, who had taught her to ride, would never forgive her for riding a lame horse, let alone one as valuable as this one. For another, she couldn't bring herself to do it. But it meant she was going to be late, which would worry some people and anger others. And it meant she would be going to her first wedding anniversary ball virtually straight from a five mile cross-country hike.

'Not that I care about that,' she muttered. 'Come on, mate!' She pulled at the reins. 'Not that I care a damn . . .' And she started to walk.

It was early twilight when she got back to the apricot pink house that was already ablaze with lights inside, and fairy lights in the garden strung between the trees.

And she ran the gauntlet of Mr and Mrs Livingstone, and Michael Smith who looked at her queerly . . .

'I'm fine! I'm sorry I'm so late but my horse cast a shoe. Has anyone arrived yet?'

'No. Oh, we were so worried about you!' Mrs Livingstone said agitatedly. 'Oh and . . .'

But Lineesa didn't wait to hear. She went up the

staircase two at a time, pulling the scarf off her hair as she went.

Her bedroom door was ajar and she closed it behind her and leant back against it breathlessly.

But she froze as a tall figure clad in a dark dinner suit and gleaming white shirt rose from one of the sherbet-green armchairs and the light gleamed on fair, faintly damp hair and a pair of blue eyes surveyed her in the same way they'd always surveyed her, derisively, assessingly, coldly and dangerously . . .

'David?' she said uncertainly and could have shot herself because her voice had quivered with a tinge of alarm.

David Marchmont said, 'Hello, Lin. Were you planning to run out on our first wedding anniversary party by any chance?'

CHAPTER TWO

SHE swallowed and twisted the aquamarine scarf between her fingers. 'No. Of course not,' she said dully, at last and pushed herself away from the door.

'Then you've left it a bit late to get ready.'

She lifted her eyes. 'Oh, I'll be ready,' she said drily.

'Yes you will, Lin,' he answered quietly and set the glass he was holding down unhurriedly. 'Even if I have to do it myself.'

'Thank-you,' her mouth was suddenly white and her hazel eyes stormy, 'but I can do it *myself*. Why don't you go down and welcome our guests in the meantime? You can tell them I won't be long.'

'Your concern for our guests is touching, if a little belated,' he murmured. 'As a matter of interest, where were you? No-one seemed to know.'

'Out,' Lineesa said starkly. 'Gone fishing only I went riding but in essence it was the same thing. I tried to escape, metaphorically of course,' she said with irony, 'from all the things I can't escape from in reality. Do you ever feel the urge to do that?'

'Frequently, my dear.' He looked at her sardonically. 'But there are some things you can't ever escape from . . .'

'David,' she interrupted urgently and painfully and clenched her hands so that her nails bit into her palms, '*please*, let me go. What you're doing . . . this farce, is achieving nothing beyond feeding a misplaced desire for revenge. The last person on

earth I wanted to hurt was Piers, I swear to
you . . .'

'You don't have to go to all that trouble, Lin.'
His eyes mocked her. 'I have—now—an inbuilt
scepticism that questions everything you say to
me. You see I'm never sure that what you're
saying is to be believed, or disbelieved. You have,
after all admitted, that upon occasions . . . you
lie . . .'

She drew a distraught breath. 'If I've told you
once, I've told you a hundred times that what I
said that night . . .'

'About younger sons and bigger fish?' he
intercepted politely, 'That bit?'

She clenched her teeth. '*Yes*. That bit . . . I was
goaded into saying that. I was angry and battling a
. . . something you wouldn't understand,' she said
bitterly. 'I was being put in my place in no
uncertain terms and I came out fighting. I . . .
retaliated, that's all it was! And I had not the
slightest idea I was being overheard, least of all by
you, Piers' older brother . . . I had no idea who
you were . . . I . . .'

'But the facts speak differently, don't they,
Lin!' he said with quiet menace. 'The facts
indicate that you led Piers a merry dance until
he didn't know whether he was coming or going,
then when he asked you to marry him, you
turned him down flat, so flat that he drove off
and killed himself.'

'It was an accident,' she whispered.

'An accident brought about by his state of
mind,' David Marchmont said mercilessly.

'If I was responsible for his state of mind, I
wasn't the only one,' she retorted in a stronger
voice. 'If you hadn't got hold of him the night
before and told him what you'd overheard and a

whole lot besides that you'd *assumed* about me, he might have understood what I tried to tell him.'

'That you hadn't been leading him a merry dance?' David Marchmont's voice was dispassionate but his cold blue eyes were contemptuous.

Lineesa took a trembling breath. 'All right,' she said huskily. 'I don't know why I still bother to try to get through to you. But just tell me this, even wrongfully convicted prisoners are allowed the privilege of knowing how long they will have to pay for their crimes, at least tell me how long my sentence is going to be . . .'

They stared at each other, she with tension stamped into every line of her body and a cold hostility in her eyes, he, quite relaxed and with a curious little smile twisting his lips.

'You have an odd conception of prisons and prisoners, my dear,' he said at last. 'Even if you do see yourself like that, you must admit you lack for nothing. Besides, this is what you wanted—the big time, so I don't see what you have to complain about. You've made it to the top. As you so rightly thought, I can give you a lot more than Piers could have. Like this for instance.' He pushed his hand into his pocket and she gasped as a river of diamonds spilled out.

He smiled and held the fabulous necklace up to the light where it glinted with an incredible radiance. 'It was my mother's. It's yours now, for as long as you stay married to me. Catch . . .'

The stones glittered like a shower of raindrops in the sun as the necklace flew through the air and landed with a soft thud at Lineesa's feet. She stared down at it, then raised her eyes.

'Happy Anniversary, Lineesa,' he murmured.

She flew at him like a tigress even although she'd sworn to herself time and time again never more to allow herself to be trapped into words or actions of mindless anger. And she had no clear idea of what she wanted to do to him beyond a compelling urge to scratch his eyes out, anything that would put just a little dent into his arrogance . . .

But she knew she'd made a mistake almost immediately, the kind of mistake she was going to pay heavily for and in the way she most hated. Knew it from the sudden glint in his narrowed eyes as he easily enough caught her arms and held them pinned behind her back in a savage grasp that threatened to crush her wrists.

'I'm never quite sure when you resort to violence, Lin, what your real intentions are,' he said through his teeth. 'You must know by now that you're no match for me this way. Is it that you think this kind of proximity with your beautiful body,' he glanced down at her heaving breasts fleetingly, 'which you so enjoyed displaying, will achieve for you what words won't? Will disarm me and have me grovelling at your feet?'

She didn't answer, just stared up at him scornfully and furiously, her face white and her lips tightly set.

'You tried that the first time we set eyes on each other, didn't you?' he murmured meditatively, not relaxing his grip in the slightest.

'Oh, you were clever about it,' he went on in the same quiet, even, detached voice. 'You looked stunned and confused like a little girl experiencing a magnetic, physical attraction for the first time. But you see I already had an inkling of the kind of professional you were. I too had seen the car ads. You were great in them, Lin. You came over so sexily it couldn't possibly have been an unconscious thing. That's why I had my doubts, you see. Which your later words confirmed . . .'

She closed her eyes and fought the pain in her wrists and shoulders, stubbornly and mutinously and thinking dimly, at least I can fight this.

But it wasn't long before she realised she was wrong and she sagged against him with a choking sound of despair, despair as much for the fact that if there was a weapon to fight David Marchmont with, she hadn't yet found it.

He released her wrists immediately and held her by her shoulders until she was steady on her feet. Then he moved away from her to pick up the diamond necklace and before she quite realised what he was about, he'd put it around her neck and turned her round to face the mirror above the fireplace.

The effect was ludicrous. Her hair was all over the place and harbouring a piece of grass and her T-shirt was dirty and sweat-stained—so was her face. And the diamonds highlighted it all so that she felt like a caricature.

Their eyes clashed in the mirror. He was standing right behind her.

She brought her hands up as if to tear the necklace off. But he spoke, not angrily, just a little drily. All the same his words stilled her hands . . .

'If you know what's good for you, Lin, and your mother, you'll wear that tonight. And you won't take too long about getting ready either. In fact you have an hour before dinner is due to be served.'

He left the room unhurriedly, closing the door quietly behind him.

She saw him go in the mirror and after a moment, removed the necklace and sank into one of the arm-chairs, to stare blankly across the room.

That's how Mrs Livingstone found her not long afterwards.

'Mrs Marchmont?' she said tentatively around the door, having knocked and received no answer. 'Mr Marchmont said you might need a hand. Shall I run a bath?'

'What? Oh. Yes, thank you, Mrs Livingstone . . .'

Lineesa soaked in the huge bath for about ten minutes and would have loved to have fallen asleep in it—the warm perfumed water was like a narcotic. But she knew she should wash her hair and that took time.

So she reluctantly took a cool shower and shampooed her hair and Mrs Livingstone offered to blow-dry it for her. 'You sit down and relax, Mrs Marchmont,' she said solicitously. 'You must be tired.'

Lineesa complied gratefully but in the end found herself wishing she was doing it herself because then she might not have had time to think back again . . .

It had been the tall, fair-haired man who'd eyed her so insolently and later so contemptuously at the party two nights previously, who had broken the news to her of Pier's death.

He'd knocked thunderously on her flat door at about eight o'clock on the morning after Piers had asked her to marry him, and when she'd opened it and stared at him with an incredulous sort of recognition in her eyes, he'd bundled her unceremoniously inside, into the living room and bodily sat her down into a chair.

Lineesa had shot up with a gulp of fear, glanced at her flat mate's bedroom and remembered with a lurch of her heart, that she'd gone away overnight. 'I . . . who . . .'

But the blue-eyed stranger who was not really a stranger had said shortly, 'Shut up and sit down!'

'No! Who the hell do you think you are?' she'd answered fiercely.

'I thought you might recognise me,' he'd shot at her with a grim smile.

'I do! But I still don't know who you are. We didn't exactly exchange names if you recall. Nor do I know why you have the right to burst in on me and . . .'

'I'm Piers' brother,' he'd interrupted and towered over her so menacingly, she'd sat down although as much from sheer, stunned surprise, as another niggle of fear.

'*Yes*, Miss Creighton . . .'

'But why . . . I don't understand,' she'd stammered.

'You will. Did Piers ask you to marry him last night?'

'Is that any business of yours?'

'*Yes*. Did he?' he'd demanded through his teeth and looked so much as if he'd like to strangle her, she'd got really frightened.

'Yes . . .'

'And what did you tell him?' What she thought of as the pair of coldest, most murderous blue eyes bored into her.

And she'd thought suddenly that she understood what was going on . . .

'You don't have to worry,' she'd said contemptuously. 'I turned him down. You know me,' she had added tauntingly, 'the girl you eavesdropped on a couple of nights ago? The girl who is after the really big time. Didn't that set your mind at rest? I presume—now, that you must have known who I was even while you didn't see fit to return the compliment . . .'

She'd stopped, realising that her voice had wound down like a faulty record because if David Marchmont had looked at her murderously before, it had been pale by comparison to the way he'd looked at her then, as if murdering was too good for her.

She'd licked her lips and found that her spurt of bravado had died.

Then he had said, 'Piers is dead . . .' And had gone on to tell her how, and exactly why he blamed her for it even when she'd all but fainted from the shock of his news.

'Stop it! Stop it!' she had cried finally, tears streaming down her white face. 'You've got it all wrong. I *loved* Piers . . . like a brother. I can't believe he's dead . . .'

'That's ironic,' he'd said harshly. 'Piers didn't believe me when I told him you were nothing but a gorgeous, grasping little tramp and that there'd be no way he could satisfy your ambitions or your appetites. He tried to tell me that underneath you were hurt and frightened but that you were coming to trust him. I'm afraid I had to laugh at that, although I refrained from telling him about the . . . way you'd looked at me, a complete stranger, the night of the party. I'm only sorry now that I didn't tell him,' he'd added viciously.

Lineesa had choked and put her hands over her ears but that hadn't shut out the remorseless voice of David Marchmont.

'Can you imagine,' he had gone on, 'how he must have felt last night when you threw his offer of marriage back in his face?'

'I didn't throw it,' she had wept. 'You don't understand anything! I told Piers right at the beginning . . .'

'Oh, come on,' he'd interrupted wearily, 'I can't

believe you're such a fool. You used Piers whatever you might have told him. You must have had some idea of what he felt for you—you can't expect me to believe you're that naive. You *used* him to pass the time and possibly advance yourself up the social ladder. And you didn't give a damn about him!'

'No, no ... Oh God!' she'd whispered distraughtly.

'And you're going to pay for that,' he'd added violently, so violently that she'd cowered back in the chair. But he hadn't touched her. In fact he'd slammed out of the flat then ...

But he'd come back two weeks later. Two weeks that had seemed like a lifetime to Lineesa, a lifetime of pain as she'd thought of Piers dead, a lifetime of accusing herself of not taking notice, not heeding her own intuition about Piers, a lifetime of knowing she would have given anything to be able to bring him back to life. In fact she'd been so wrapped up in her agony for Piers she hadn't given David Marchmont much thought other than to vaguely surmise that what he'd said and the way he'd acted had sprung from a well of grief ...

So it was that she'd almost fainted again when he'd returned to the flat one wet evening when she was again alone, and outlined to her exactly how she was going to pay for Piers' death.

'M-marry you!' she'd stammered. 'You must be mad ...'

He'd smiled slightly, the coldest smile she'd ever seen. 'Not at all,' he'd drawled. 'You wanted the big time—you've got it.'

'I ... I wouldn't marry you if you were the last man on earth!'

'Yes you will, Lineesa. May I call you that?'

'You can call me what you like but it won't

make me want to marry you ...' She'd stared at him shakenly, desperately trying to plot this course of events and feeling a cold finger of fear touching her heart.

'It's not so much a question of wanting to,' he'd corrected smoothly, 'although I'd be surprised if you didn't change your mind in time. No, at present it's a question of having no choice. Shall I tell you why?'

He'd told her. Apparently he was a director of the company which had financed the mortgage on Lineesa's mother's house. And thereby in the position of foreclosing on that mortgage.

'No you're not!' she'd protested vigorously. 'While I'm in the position to keep up the repayments you can't do that and if you try to, I'll take you court!'

'Well, that's going to be the problem, my dear Lineesa. If you don't marry me I shall personally see to it that you never get another modelling assignment and don't think I couldn't do that because it would only take a word from me in a few ears ...'

'You bastard,' she'd whispered. 'You wouldn't ...'

'Yes I would. And the thing is, without a job, how *would* you be able to keep up the repayments on that mortgage?'

'I ... could take you to court for *that*! There's got to be a law against it ...'

'There is. It's called defamation of character basically, although you might have a hard time getting anyone to stand up in court to testify to the fact that they allowed me to sway them over the matter of using you to advertise their products. You're welcome to try, however. But I don't suppose your mother would enjoy that. Because,

however much it cost me, I wouldn't mind in the
least, standing up in a court of law and telling the
world why I had defamed you, down to the last
detail.'

'You are mad,' she'd said. 'How . . .'

'Do I know so much about your mother?' he'd
supplied. 'I made it my business to know, that's
how. Did *you* know she's been seeing a doctor
lately. On account of her heart?'

'*What?*'

'You didn't. She told a friend of hers at the
bridge club that she didn't want to worry you . . .
She's very proud of you, Lineesa. She tells all her
friends that you're so different from most girls,
specially those girls in your line of business. She
points to her house and says—my daughter earned
that for me. I don't suppose she realises that you
might have earned a lot of it flat on your back
because I think she *is* really naïve . . .'

And that had been the first time Lineesa had
launched herself at David Marchmont intent on
God knows what. Only to end up ignominiously in
his arms, panting with fury and frustration. But
three months later, she'd married him as he'd
predicted, because his threats had begun to come
all too true, her work load had mysteriously and
drastically begun to lighten, and her mother's
doctor had confirmed that her mother had a heart
problem and that a sense of peace and security and
lack of strain could be vital.

But on her wedding night, Lineesa had suffered
another shock. She'd anticipated just how she
would pay and had said tightly, 'All right, let's get
it over and done with.'

David Marchmont had watched her carefully
across the sumptuous lounge of the hotel suite.
She'd showered and changed into a nightgown and

a sherry-coloured velvet robe. She'd left her hair loose and had made one decision, one only since having had a plain gold wedding band placed on her left hand, that if she died doing it, there was no way she'd let this tall man who was now her husband, see how frightened of him she really was.

He'd pulled his tie off then and slung his jacket across the back of a chair—he'd been on the 'phone, while she'd changed. A business call she'd gathered and smiled to herself ironically.

'Get what over with?' he'd enquired finally and turned to the bar to pour two glasses of champagne from the bottle in the silver bucket which had been sent up to the suite with the compliments of the management. 'Cheers,' he'd added with a hatefully mocking smile twisting his lips as he'd handed her a glass. 'Why don't you sit down?'

She'd sat down and sipped her champagne and he'd done likewise, opposite her with one hand shoved into his trouser pocket and his long legs sprawled out.

'Get what over and done with?' he'd said again, idly.

'I think you must know what I mean,' she'd murmured.

He'd smiled slightly and her heart had started to beat heavily and her mouth had gone dry.

'Why don't you demonstrate what you mean? So that there can be no misunderstandings?' he'd remarked blandly then.

She'd set her teeth. 'Look,' her voice had quivered, 'I don't understand why you're trying to beat about the bush—I don't know if it's all part of the plan . . .'

'As a matter of fact it's not,' he'd interrupted amusedly. 'Taking you to bed was the last thing I had in mind. I'm sorry if that inconveniences you but I believe cold showers are—efficacious in those circumstances.'

Lineesa's mouth had dropped open but her sense of stunning though incredulous relief at his earlier sentiments had been almost equalled by a blazing anger at his last words. All of which had mingled powerfully and contrived to keep her rooted to her seat for several minutes. She'd looked down at the glass in her hand and wondered briefly if anyone had ever been brained by a champagne glass. And had finally said in a strained difficult voice, 'Please don't misunderstand this too, but would you mind telling me why you . . . *forced* me to marry you if . . .'

'If I didn't want to sleep with you? Very well, I will.' His voice had hardened and all the sardonic amusement had fled from his eyes. 'This is the big time you so hankered for, Lineesa. But you're going to learn that when you're an empty, shallow, mercenary little tart with no feelings, you will be treated as such too. You're going to be Mrs David Marchmont in *name* only, for as long as I see fit to keep you that way. You're going to be a useless though undeniably very decorative,' his eyes had glittered cruelly, 'ornament. You may have all the clothes you desire and the trinkets that might appeal to your avaricious little heart, you'll have the social standing of being my wife but you'll come and go where and when I tell you to and you'll jump to any tune I care to call. And there's one thing you will not do, unless you wish your mother to hear about it, you will not throw your lures out to any other man . . . Oh, and by the way, don't bother trying it again on me either, you're wasting your time.'

Lineesa had gone as white as a sheet of paper as

he'd spoken. And she'd jumped up when he'd
finished and tried to speak. 'You ... you're
diabolical! You can't ... I ...'

'But I have,' he'd answered quietly. 'You
thought you could buy all this with your body,
and that you could ride rough-shod over anyone in
the process. But you made one mistake, you
shouldn't have done it to *my* brother. I suppose
you thought too that that perfect face and figure
would bring me round as well. But I have to tell
you that all it's earned you this time is a lesson in
being ridden over rough-shod, yourself ...'

'... Mrs Marchmont?'

Mrs Livingstone's voice penetrated Lineesa's
consciousness from a long way away.

'What?' she said vaguely.

'Your hair is just about dry. And we're running
out of time ...'

Lineesa trembled. Then she said quietly, 'Of
course ...

'Which dress will you wear?'

'The ... black one I think. It will go well with
the diamonds.'

'My dear Lin! You look stunning! But you always
do!'

Dinner was over and the ball guests were
arriving. Lineesa glinted a smile at her brother-in-
law and murmured 'Thank-you, Simon.'

'I didn't get a chance to tell you earlier. Sorry to
hear about your horse but if I can pass on a little
secret of mine—antiphlogistine! Good evening,' he
broke off to say genially to an arriving couple
who'd just shaken Lineesa's hand. 'What was I
saying? Oh yes, antiphlogistine. As a poultice for
a bruise it's ...'

'It is not!' Lineesa's sister-in-law, Bronwen interrupted. 'I must say you look fabulous, Lin. As I've no doubt Simon's been telling you! But for my book, nothing can beat a poultice of bran, linseed oil and hot water. Hello there!' she added to another group of arriving guests.

'My dear Bronwen,' Simon, who was as tall and dark as his wife was short and fair, said laughingly, 'I thought you'd turned your attention to dogs these days.'

'I have,' his very pregnant wife replied darkly. 'You may not have noticed that I'm not in any condition to be having much to do with horses at the moment. Nor have I been at regular intervals over the past five years. Which is the only reason I turned to dogs. But that doesn't mean I've forgotten about poultices and things.'

'Darling,' Simon said cheerfully, 'if you're cross with me because you're not as sylph-like as many of the ladies present tonight, may I tell you yet again that I adore you when you're pregnant.'

'I don't see how you can,' Bronwen replied candidly and looked down at herself ruefully. 'I mean I can't even see my feet. And when you've got someone like Lin to look at . . .'

'Dear heart, one of these fine days, Lin will look like you do and David will be able to corroborate how *I* feel . . . won't you, mate?' Simon said as David Marchmont appeared at his side.

'Won't I what?'

'Be able to demonstrate that Lin's not only there to be looked at and . . .'

'*Simon!*' Bronwen said exasperatedly. 'Do forgive him, Lin,' she added as Lineesa's cheeks coloured faintly. 'He doesn't really mean to be . . . indelicate, at least I don't think he does but . . .'

The band struck up at that point and David

interrupted his sister with a faintly wry smile, 'Shall we set the ball rolling? Mrs Marchmont,' he turned to Lineesa. 'I believe this is our dance . . .'

Lineesa moved into his arms obediently but there was a shimmer of unshed tears in her hazel eyes as she glanced up at him briefly for Simon's words had hit home in a way he'd probably never meant them to, never dreamt they would.

'My brother-in-law was never noted for his tact,' David Marchmont said.

Lineesa didn't answer, just concentrated on what her feet were doing.

'Don't play dumb with me, Lin.' The words were softly spoken but imperative all the same.

She took a breath and blinked. And the tears were gone when she looked up, and her eyes defiant. 'I don't suppose it was such a tactless thing to say in the normal course of events. It only became tactless when applied to me but he wasn't to know that.'

'No. He wasn't,' he said after a moment. 'I'm only surprised you were so affected by his . . . lack of tact.'

'That's because you've never once accredited me with any feelings, probably.' She looked at him expressionlessly then turned her head away deliberately.

They danced in silence for a while and gradually the floor began to fill up. Marchmont was not possessed of a ballroom but the main lounge was an enormous room that lent itself well to dancing. Most of the furniture had been removed and the wooden floor stripped of its Persian carpets. The band had supplied its own dais and the very high ceiling of the room provided good acoustics. And the brilliant colours of many a beautiful dress

looked good against the panelled walls that were
the main feature of the lounge.

Then he said, 'The necklace goes well with that
dress. Or rather, it goes well with your skin . . .'

Lineesa shivered involuntarily and wondered
just how much more she could take in one night.
Yet it had been a deliberate action, she knew, to
wear this dress. She'd worn it once before and he'd
looked her up and down critically and asked her
coolly why she bothered to wear anything at all.
And on that occasion she'd pointed to ninety per
cent of the females present and demanded to know
what was so different about her dress. He'd replied
that it must have something to do with the wearer.

And again tonight there were as many women in
strapless backless evening gowns as had been the
time before . . . Not that her dress was either
strapless or backless but the glittering black sheath
fitted her perfectly and the bodice hugged her
breasts like a second skin but revealed nothing
more than the faint shadow of where the valley
between her breasts began. But it was true that the
straps that held it up were thin, and that the
golden, delicately tanned skin of her shoulders and
arms was bare. And tonight it was true that the
pendant stone of the diamond necklace lay like a
trembling teardrop in that shadowed valley.

It was also true that Lineesa had planned to
wear something quite different tonight, a dress
she'd had specially made for the occasion which
was positively demure. And yet, she'd allowed
herself to be goaded into changing her mind,
knowing full well what his reaction would be . . .

'Once a tart, always a tart, I suppose,' she
murmured huskily and smiled up at him as he
swung her around to the music. 'But I'll go up and
change if you like. Just say the word,' she added

ironically. 'You must admit I'm a very biddable tart . . . for the most part.'

He smiled back at her with his lips but not his eyes. In fact she shivered again at what she saw in his eyes and stumbled unaccountably so that he gathered her close to him, so close that her body was moulded against his in an iron grip that crushed her breasts and made her feel soft and slight and supremely vulnerable in a curious way. And her eyes flew to his in an unguarded way that she couldn't help, couldn't understand or perhaps didn't want to understand . . .

And he laughed at the sudden rush of colour that poured into her cheeks. Laughed and loosened his hold. 'How right you are, Lin. You never learn do you?' he drawled. 'No,' he said as she moved convulsively, 'you can't hit me, as much as I know you'd love to, my beautiful lady-wife . . .'

'I don't want to hit you . . . Just let me go,' she whispered through her teeth.

'When the dance is over,' he said mildly. 'There . . .'

They came to a standstill as the music stopped but he didn't immediately let her go. Instead he drew her slender hand up between them and bent his head to touch his lips to it briefly. 'You're free to play the lady of the manor now, as our guests expect you to and I expect you to. That must be some compensation surely for all the grievances you fancy you cherish against me. To be in the position to be a lady, so called?' His blue eyes mocked her. 'See you later, sweetheart,' he said and kissed her hand again before releasing it.

But a burst of applause surprised them both— particularly Lineesa who looked around and blinked to see most of their guests gathered in a loose circle around them. Then the band burst forth into an impromptu rendition of *Happy Birthday* and everyone began to sing although they adapted the words to suit the occasion. Then someone called out, 'Give her a real kiss, David!'

Lineesa tensed but David Marchmont smiled down at her with genuine amusement. And he brought his hands up to cup her shoulders. 'Don't disappoint them,' he murmured barely audibly.

She hesitated, then closed her eyes and lifted her face mutely, never for one moment imagining that he would do more than brush her lips with his own as he'd done to her hand. But his fingers tightened on her shoulders briefly then he slid his arms around her and pulled her close again and his lips were insistent as they found hers so that she parted them involuntarily and found herself being kissed thoroughly by the man who had gone out of his way to hurt and humiliate her ever since he'd first laid eyes on her.

And when it was over, he still held her in his arms to a chorus of delighted approval as she stared up at him, unbelievingly, stunned . . .

Until he released her abruptly and they were deluged by people shaking their hands and wishing them many more years of happiness.

I think I might get drunk, Lineesa thought, as she smiled and murmured she knew not what, and was kissed and patted fondly. Then there was a lull and Cathy Corbett stood in front of her looking magnificent in scarlet and gold—a sort of sari affair.

Lineesa automatically put out her hand but Cathy merely glanced at it with her dark, dark eyes and smiled.

'Congratulations, Lin,' she said softly. 'You and David are great actors.'

Lineesa dropped her hand. 'Are we?' she murmured.

'Yes, you are . . .'

'Cathy,' Lineesa said patiently, 'this could become one of those funny conversations—I could say what do you mean? And I suppose you could say something to the effect that I must know what you mean. And I could say no, I don't and you could say . . .' She shrugged. 'We could go on all night!'

'You think you're so clever, don't you, Lin?' Cathy retorted after a pregnant little pause.

'No. I don't,' Lineesa said calmly and smiled faintly. 'Here we go again! If there's something you'd like to say to me, why not come straight out with it?'

'But you *know* it, Lin,' Cathy retorted and let her eyes rest lingeringly on David who'd moved out of earshot a few minutes earlier. 'That's why you're trying to tie me in knots . . .'

'Heaven forbid!' Lineesa answered wearily and thought of adding something cutting like . . . for someone who has such an aversion to people only using their bodies, I can't imagine why David is sleeping with you, Cathy!

Yet she didn't. Instead, she said formally, 'I hope you enjoy being at Marchmont, Cathy. Will you excuse me?'

But as she turned away, she thought, *hell*, I think I will get drunk. It beats getting sick—well, it beats being sickened by that gloating, basically dumb . . . how could he? After all he's said to me and the way he's treated me? And he must have known some spiteful know-alls would fall over themselves to tell me that he's been seen frequently in Cathy Corbett's company. I could have stood anyone but her . . .

But the next three hours did not provide the opportunity to get drunk, not that Lineesa had seriously planned to do it, but as she circulated and danced and conversed, she began to feel distinctly not with it. Then her energy ran out abruptly and she knew she could not pass another smiling, inane remark or dance another dance for all the tea in China. And she collared a waiter from the catering company and extracted a long, frosted glass from his tray, and slipped away with it to a dark deserted corner of the terrace.

The moon was a pale slice of light and its reflection was cutting a swathe of silver across the waters of the Hawkesbury, and the night air was refreshingly cool.

So was the drink she was sipping which was, she discovered, a Margarita, a blend of tequila, lemon and salt. Bronwen's partial to these, she thought, and smiled faintly.

It had in fact, never ceased to amaze Lineesa how well David's sister had accepted her. She'd expected to meet some initial resistance at least, to David marrying her of all people and so soon after Piers' death. But if Bronwen St John had known that Lineesa had been going out with her younger brother first, she'd never given any indication of it. Nor had she by so much as a word or a look, ever indicated that she was aware of what probably more and more people were coming to realise— that her elder brother's marriage was not quite your common or garden species of marriage.

But as Lineesa had got to know her, she'd realised that Bronwen and Simon St John lived in a world of their own that rarely strayed across the boundaries of their twenty acre property at Richmond, west of Sydney, where they bred horses and dogs—and children, the current one due being the fourth in a line of little St Johns. Simon, a dedicated horseman and top polo player was possessed of private means which allowed him, as far as Lineesa could see, to very seldom think or talk about anything but horses. Not that Bronwen seemed to mind, being similarly inclined herself. In fact they appeared to be ideally matched and if you could force your way into their house, the untidiest abode Lineesa had ever come across, you were met by a spirit of love and laughter that tended to melt away the mess.

Not that Lineesa visited often. She felt too much of a fraud to expose herself to being called Aunty Lin frequently, and doted on by two little girls and one small boy who not only bore his dead uncle's name but his eyes and shape of face too.

It's strange she thought, as she sipped her Margarita, apart from the fact that they're all fair, there's hardly anything in Bronwen that reminds me of Piers, and nothing in David yet . . .

'. . . Mrs Marchmont?'

A voice spoke out of the darkness behind her.

She jumped and spilled some of her drink, and turned to stare through the gloom. 'Who is it?'

'Michael Smith, Mrs Marchmont.'

'Oh . . .' Lineesa relaxed and found she could make out his tall, thin form. 'You gave me a fright. Are you checking up on me?'

'Not at all, Mrs Marchmont.'

'I wouldn't be surprised if you were, nor would I be cross,' she said conversationally. 'It's all part of your job, isn't it?'

'Not to check up on you, ma'am,' he replied with dignity although also sounding just a little hurt.

'Well, I mean you're at every party and so on . . .'

'Only to see that things run smoothly. Which

they have tonight despite...' He broke off abruptly.

'Despite me,' she said drily. 'Yes. But don't you get insanely bored? I mean, how awful can it be seeing that other people's parties run smoothly? Have you ever,' she smiled suddenly, 'thought of running amok and gate-crashing the occasion? Becoming whatever the male version of the belle of the ball is?'

'Yes,' he said and took a breath.

Lineesa turned her head. 'I'm glad,' she said softly.

'Glad?' He sounded immensely surprised. 'Why?'

'Because it proves you're human, I suppose.'

'Did you ... think I wasn't?' he asked awkwardly.

'Oh, not really! But you are so super efficient, it's sometimes quite easy to think of you as having no feelings, no ...' she grimaced inwardly and wondered why she'd got herself into this conversation, 'uh, I guess it's just that you're very good at your job,' she finished a little lamely.

He was silent for a time, in fact so long, Lineesa looked around finally, and got the shock of her life. Because Michael Smith had moved a step forward so that the verandah above was no longer shading his face from the moonlight and on it she saw such a look of naked, suffering, longing directed squarely at her, she flinched visibly. And in the moment that he realised what she must have seen on his face and put his hand up to grab his spectacles in a gesture of utter, miserable confusion, a lot of little things fell into place for Lineesa.

How could I have been so blind? she wondered in a sudden agony of remorse that was as intense as Michael Smith's misery. But I've done nothing to encourage him or . . .

She tensed as a step was heard along the terrace and David materialised out of the thin shadows.

'Well, well,' he drawled as he came up to them. 'I wondered where you'd got to, Lin. I might have expected to find you . . .'

Both Lineesa and Michael Smith broke in then to each utter something disjointed and as their words clashed unintelligibly and fell like stones into a pool of silence, David Marchmont smiled a curious little smile and then he said, 'I see . . . Well, I don't think we need your services anymore tonight, Mike. Thank-you for all you've done. I think I mentioned that I'd be flying up to Karendale on Monday and I expect to stay the week so you can have a much deserved break. See you then, mate.'

Michael Smith looked slightly dazed, as if he wasn't sure what was real and what was imagined. Then he mumbled something and stepped indoors.

'If you think . . .' Lineesa began.

'I'll tell you what I think, Lin,' David said coldly, 'at a more appropriate moment. In the meantime, people are beginning to leave, those staying need their hostess to say good night to them at least—all of which we shall do together.'

He was as good as his word. He never left her side until at last the big house was quiet. Then he followed her upstairs and into the apricot bedroom and closed the door with a kind of purpose and finality that made her tighten her lips outwardly but feel cold inwardly . . .

CHAPTER THREE

THEY stared at each other for a few moments.

Then she said tautly, 'If you're planning to read me the riot act, David, you'll be wasting your breath. For one thing I'm *tired*!'

'That wasn't precisely what I had in mind,' he murmured. 'But since you mentioned it perhaps I'll just say this. You can't help yourself, can you, Lin? You learnt *nothing* from what happened to Piers. You couldn't have, otherwise you wouldn't now be playing ducks and drakes with Mike's emotions . . .'

She sucked in a furious breath. 'I had no *idea* he felt like that about me. I . . . it only dawned on me for the first time tonight. As for encouraging him or playing ducks and drakes with his emotions . . .'

'Then what were you doing alone with him outside in the moonlight? Being platonic? He looked about as unplatonic in a confused, embarrassed, guilt-laden way as only a man who has been led on where he knows he shouldn't tread, can.'

'No!' she whispered distraughtly, 'You've got it all wrong—as usual.'

'Then why don't you put me right?' he said gently but with his eyes glinting sardonically.

'He *was* embarrassed because . . . oh, hell,' she said and rubbed her temples wearily. 'You're not going to believe a word I say so why should I bother? You never do . . .'

'I seem to recall going through all that earlier this evening,' he said drily.

'We did,' she answered tensely. 'It's your favourite topic of discussion in my company. I mean, this is only just an extension of that old subject, isn't it? What a cruel, heartless bitch I am and how I lure unsuspecting, *decent* young men into my toils only to spurn them . . . oh God!' she said passionately and realised suddenly that she was crying, a thing she hadn't done since Piers' death, 'if you only knew how I wish I'd never laid eyes on any man, young or old, decent or otherwise, if you only knew how right my mother was . . .'

She sank down into one of the armchairs and wept into her hands with an intensity that was totally beyond her control, that actually hurt physically.

Until he pulled her to her feet and said harshly, 'Stop it, Lin. You'll make yourself sick.'

'Do you think I care?' she gulped. 'Do you think I don't often wonder if I wouldn't be better off dead? Better me than Piers . . .'

'You're hysterical,' he said quietly. 'And overtired perhaps.' He studied her critically.

'Y-yes,' she whispered bitterly and drew a shuddering breath. 'Of course . . .' She wiped her nose with the back of her hand and then wiped her eyes with her forearm.

'Would you,' he hesitated briefly, 'like something to help get to sleep?'

'What?' she said dully.

'A stiff scotch . . .'

'Why not? I had thought of getting drunk earlier in the evening funnily enough. I'm only sorry I didn't now. But I'll get it . . .'

'You get yourself into bed,' he said. 'I'll be back.'

The door closed and Lineesa shrugged and

began to do as she was bid—you see I am
biddable, she thought light-headedly . . .

But however biddable, she was not in bed when
David reappeared, nor was she changed. In fact
she was struggling to undo the diamond necklace
and getting quite frantic in the process.

'What's wrong?' he said with a frown as he put
not a scotch but a glass of milk and a tablet on the
bedside table.

'Your mother's bloody necklace,' she answered
tensely. 'The catch must have jammed or something. I can't get it off.'

'You'll break it if you handle it like that,' he
said dryly.

'Well I'd rather break it than have to wear it
around my neck like a chain, forever!' Her voice
rose and to her horror she started to cry again and
she ground her teeth in futility and despair and
yanked the necklace furiously but to no avail.

'Stop it, Lin,' he said sharply and for the second
time that night. 'Let me do it.'

His fingers were cool on the back of her neck
and she shivered miserably and then found she
couldn't stop shivering and shaking like an idiot
even when the necklace came off quite easily and
he pushed it into his pocket and turned her round
to face him. His blue eyes were narrowed and
watchful as he studied her again for a long
moment, during which she made a concerted effort
to pull herself together but more tears streamed
down her face and she couldn't stop shaking.

'I think I'll get Mrs Livingstone to help you to
bed,' he said finally.

'No!' she gasped. 'I can manage . . . I don't want
her to see me like this . . .' Her voice died away.

'Then you'll have to put up with me doing it
because I don't think you can manage it . . .'

'*No.*' She spat the word out and moved away but she tripped and would have fallen if he hadn't caught her. 'Go away,' she panted as he lifted her up into his arms and took her over to the bed. 'Just go *away*. I'm fine.'

'So I see,' he said emotionlessly and turned her round. 'Does this dress have a zip? Ah, yes . . .'

'*David* . . .'

'Shut up, Lin,' he said mercilessly as he slid the straps off her shoulder and the dress fell down to her waist. Then he slid his fingers between her skin and the back of her black, strapless bra and undid the fastening. She gasped again and brought her hands up furiously, to cover herself and fight him off at the same time but he simply bore her hands down to her sides and turned her round to face him, and sat her down.

'This isn't a time for false modesty,' he murmured as the bra fell into her lap. 'Where's your nightgown?'

She stared up at him, speechless, naked to the waist and more embarrassed, more humiliated than she'd ever been by anything he'd ever done to her.

But if he noticed it he gave no sign. In fact his eyes were completely impersonal as he looked down at her enquiringly.

'U-under the pillow,' she whispered and closed her eyes as her head sank down and her hair fell forward to hide her face and cover her breasts.

'Got it,' he said a moment later. 'Lin?'

She lifted her head so that he could slide the white silk on to her and obediently slid her arms into the armholes. But as he stood her up and the cloud of white slid down her body, she said huskily, 'I can do the rest . . .'

She pulled off her shoes, then her dress and her

pantyhose. And she didn't look at him as she walked unsteadily round the bed, her body clearly outlined in the lamplight beneath the same nightgown that had revealed it in the sunlight that morning . . . a lifetime away, she thought dimly.

The sheets were cool as she slid between them and her hair splayed out on the pillow as she stared up at the ceiling blankly.

And she jumped when he said, 'Take this, Lin,' as if she'd forgotten he was still there.

'What?'

'This. It's a sleeping pill, only a mild one. I got it from Mrs Livingstone. She's an insomniac apparently.'

'Yes.' She raised her head. 'She told me once . . .'

'Sit up,' he said patiently. 'I would have had the milk warmed up, but she said you loath warm milk.'

'Yes . . . I don't remember telling her that . . .'

'Drink it all . . .'

She swallowed the pill and drank the milk and then lay back without once looking at him. 'I wonder how long it takes to work,' she murmured. 'Not long I hope.' And felt those weak, foolish tears well again so she pulled the spare pillow into her arms and buried her face in it.

He said nothing, just watched her sombrely as her shoulder shook convulsively. Then he sat down beside her and stroked her hair gently.

She stiffened at first but there was no real fight left in her. And finally she quietened and began to feel drowsy. And she fell asleep thinking that the real reason she hated David Marchmont so much was . . . was . . .

But the sleeping pill had finally done its work. And she didn't know that he prised the pillow out of her arms gently and pulled the coverlet over her. Nor did she know that he sat watching her for a long time and then, that for the first time since coming to Marchmont, the inter-connecting door between their bedrooms was opened and stayed open all night.

In fact the next thing she knew was that someone was calling her name and when she finally opened her eyes it was to see what appeared to be a doctor sitting beside her on the bed.

'... Mrs Marchmont? Ah, you're awake,' the man with the stethoscope around his neck said quietly.

She blinked uncertainly. 'Is ... something wrong?'

'I don't think so. By the way I'm Trevor White. How do you do? No, I don't think anything is wrong but you have thrown everyone into a bit of a panic, you see.'

'I ... have?' Lineesa frowned and tried to sit up.

'Mmm. You've slept rather a long time.'

'What is the time?'

'Five o'clock.'

Lineesa stared at him.

'In the afternoon,' he added. 'That is a fair haul—from roughly two-thirty in the morning according to David here.'

Her eyes widened and for the first time since waking up she realised David was standing behind this strange man.

'I ... I couldn't have slept that long. There must be some mistake,' she said foolishly feeling totally disorientated and not even able to remember falling asleep.

'Well, you were rather tired,' Trevor White said patiently and gently. 'If you remember, there was a ball last night ...'

Lineesa closed her eyes as everything fell into place. She sighed and rubbed her face. 'Oh . . . yes,' she said wearily. 'I remember now. But I took a sleeping pill too.' Her eyes jerked to David's in sudden alarm. 'What's happened to . . . everyone?'

He spoke for the first time. 'Don't worry about them.'

'But the picnic . . .'

He smiled slightly. 'It's been pouring with rain all day. They were all happy enough to go home at lunch time. Lin, I'd like you to let Trevor give you a thorough examination while he's here. It's not like you,' he hesitated, 'to tire so easily . . .'

'You could have woken me up,' she interrupted.

'That's not the point,' he said a touch grimly.

'But I'm fine,' she protested. 'I . . .'

'All the same, it won't do any harm. I'll leave you two to it,' he said and left the room, giving her no chance to argue further.

'David hasn't changed,' Trevor White said with a grin.

'You know him? I mean you're not just a doctor he called in?'

'No. Well, I am the doctor he called in but I've known David for years. We went to school together. He was rather autocratic even in those days. Now don't tell him I told you that!' He smiled at her conspiratorially, and she thought that he had nice brown eyes.

She even found herself smiling back. But it faded almost immediately and she said gravely, 'Really, there's nothing wrong with me.'

'How would it be if I gave you the once over and then we could both tell David that? He might believe us.'

She sighed. 'All right . . .'

'Mmm,' he said some time later after meticulously checking her blood pressure, her pulse, her heart-beat, her ears, nose and throat and looking into her pupils with a light, 'so far so good.'

'I told you,' she murmured. 'Do you often get called out for people who over-sleep?'

'No. Life would be simpler if I did. May I ask you a few questions?' He smiled at her reassuringly and she nodded.

'Are you pregnant?'

'No . . .'

'Sometimes one doesn't know very early on . . .'

'No I'm not,' she said definitely.

'Then are you worried or upset about something?' The question was delivered in the same easy tones and it took her by surprise.

'I . . . what do you mean?' she asked a little breathlessly and wondered for a fleeting moment if David had told him . . . No, she thought immediately, he wouldn't do that. Although he might have mentioned what a state I was in last night. But then he must know why . . .

Trevor White said, 'When you're carrying some sort of a mental burden, and it can happen to most of us that things just get too much for us from time to time, then your body can take over.'

How right you are, she marvelled, but to herself. That's exactly what must have happened. I slept and slept because I didn't want to face up to anymore of . . .

She looked at Trevor White with his nice brown eyes and warm smile and easy manner, but who was also a friend of David's and thought, if you weren't a friend of his, I could tell you about my problems. But what would be the use, anyway? You couldn't do anything—no-one can. And because you *are* a friend of his there's no way I can tell you. David must know that too. In fact

David must know what's wrong with me so why all this fuss? Could he be suffering from a guilty conscience? I doubt that, she thought ironically. I'm the one with the guilty conscience ... Perhaps he simply wants to see me fighting fit for the next bout of hostilities he has planned ...

'Mrs Marchmont?'

'Oh.' Lineesa came out of her bitter thoughts and glanced up at the doctor. 'Yes—I mean, no, I have no burdens but yes, I think you were right about the body taking over.' She managed a sort of smile. 'You see I don't think anyone realised just how far I had to walk yesterday after my horse cast a shoe, but that was my fault. In the rush when I did get home, I didn't really tell anyone. Then there was the ball ... I really think I was just overtired.'

He looked at her thoughtfully for a moment. Then he said, 'Maybe. Although I'm told you're exceptionally fit. You swim and ride and walk a lot ...'

Lineesa sighed inwardly. 'Doctor ...'

'Trevor,' he said. 'I'm almost one of the family, you know. I've delivered all of Bronwen's babies.'

'Trevor then ...'

'Could that be the problem?' he interrupted.

She frowned bewilderedly. 'Bronwen's babies?'

'Not *per se*. But if you'd hoped to fall pregnant by now?'

Lineesa closed her eyes. 'It's not that,' she said tiredly. 'It's not *anything*, believe me. Well, it's nothing more than a case of over-exerting myself yesterday. I really think this is crazy,' she added intensely. 'I have to be surprised you're going along with it.'

'All right,' he answered mildly and began to pack his bag.

'Do you believe me?'

He hesitated. 'I think that physically, you're fine.'

'What will you tell David?' she asked a shade warily.

'That, but ... how long since you two had a holiday? A proper holiday far, far from the madding crowd?'

Lineesa opened her mouth but shut it almost immediately.

'Would you mind if I suggested a break for you?' he said persuasively.

A break, she thought, and almost smiled. A holiday with David would be like being sentenced to hard labour. Not that he'd want to take a holiday with me. But ...

She moved her hands restlessly at what she was thinking. Would he let me go away for a while on my own? Anywhere, I don't care where. Just somewhere I could—be alone.

'A ... break would be nice,' she murmured.

'Good. I'll see what I can do,' Trevor White replied.

The house was very quiet. Lineesa lay in bed and heard a car drive away and presumed it was the doctor leaving.

I wonder if he persuaded David to let me have a break, she mused. I should get up ...

But the lethargy that seemed to have invaded her, held her captive still. She looked at her bedside clock. It was now six o'clock. Is there any point? she wondered. Is there any point to anything any more? It's been twelve months—and one day. A lost day! Twelve months of being ... an ornament. I've achieved nothing in a year. Nothing. That's a long time ... Oh, I've *done* a lot. I've—held a very successful champagne luncheon in the car park at Flemington race-course on Melbourne Cup day, plus getting my photo in the papers and women's magazine for being so well-dressed that day. I've presided over dinner parties, house parties, yacht parties ... parties, parties and more parties. I've been seen at other people's parties too, and I've been to all the right premières and I've been delivered to and fro to all these dazzling engagements like a puppet. And my poor mother is quite bedazzled by my success although she still sometimes gets mixed up when she's tired and marvels at how lucky I was to fall for one brother and then the other! But she's lapping it up all the same and on account of me is the most prestigious member of her bridge club. And if I sometimes worry about her health, at least I know she's happy ...

Then there's been Marchmont. It hasn't been all bad. Mr Livingstone taught me to ride and Mrs Livingstone ... well, I think she likes me. She did say once that compared to the last Mrs Marchmont, I was a breeze. David's mother was a bit of a tartar, I gather. Piers' mother—for that matter Bronwen's mother ... A lady with a mind like a steel trap and a tongue like a hatchet ... no, Mrs Livingstone didn't say that. Who did? Piers ... he much preferred his father, he said. Oh Piers ...

'Lin?'

She jumped. It was David with a tray in his hands.

'Oh, look I can get up!' she protested. 'There's nothing wrong with me.'

'You'll do no such thing, Mrs Marchmont,' Mrs Livingstone said strongly as she bustled in behind David with an armful of pillows. 'Here. Let me bolster you up. That's better! Now—put the tray down here, Mr David—it's nothing heavy, Mrs Marchmont,' she said very seriously to Lineesa. 'Just a fish soup, and an omlette to follow. I wish you'd told me!' she added and although her once dark hair was now grey, her snapping dark eyes had lost none of their fire. 'I knew you were tired last night when I was helping you to dress. I could just feel that your heart wasn't in it. But I thought you'd come right. You should have told me you weren't up to it!'

'But I was,' Lineesa protested. She glanced at David. He was casually dressed in cream linen trousers and a cream T-shirt that was open at the throat and his brown leather belt matched the gleaming leather of his hand-made shoes. He looked sleek and, although his face was unreadable, as infinitely dangerous as he always did, to her. A man who was still a mystery to her in lots of ways. An attractive man to many women, she knew, who had a side of him that could be amusing, provocative, sometimes surprisingly sensitive and often quite kind. Yet that side of David Marchmont was never shown to her, she only knew it existed indirectly from observing him with other people. What he showed to her was quite a different thing, a relentlessness and an unmerciful scorn that chilled her to the soul and made her feel helpless and hopeless . . .

She sighed inwardly. 'Anyway, it was a bit late to cancel it,' she murmured as Mrs Livingstone fussed over her and positioned the special tray that had legs for an invalid bed, just so. And she found that her thoughts had taken away any appetite she might have had so that the deliciously fragrant food set before her made her feel like a reluctant mountain climber sent out to conquer Everest.

'Now get some food into you, Mrs Marchmont,' Mrs Livingstone commanded and cast a speaking look at David just before she bustled out.

'I couldn't possibly eat all this,' Lineesa said huskily into the silence Mrs Livingstone's departure had left in its wake. 'Have you eaten?'

He looked at her meditatively for a moment and she was suddenly drearily conscious that she must look a mess. Then he pulled one of the armchairs over to the side of the bed and sat down. 'Eat, Lin,' he said quietly and reached across to unfurl the napkin on the tray and hand it to her.

She took a deep breath and thought of creating a small mutiny—he couldn't force her to eat, after all. That was one thing he couldn't do . . .

'Mrs Livingstone went to a lot of trouble to make something you would like,' he said as if reading her mind.

Their glances clashed but the expression in his blue eyes was only faintly wry and she immediately felt like a troublesome child. But I suppose it is childish, she thought wearily and picked up her spoon.

He didn't speak until she'd finished the soup and most of the omlette. Then he removed the tray and poured her a cup of coffee.

'How do you feel?' he said.

'All right. There's nothing wrong with me.' She sipped her coffee and avoided his eyes.

'What about what happened last night?' he queried after a moment.

'What about it?' she answered flatly.

'You were highly distraught, if you recall,' he murmured.

'Was I? I can't imagine why. I should be so used to having those kind of accusations levelled at me, you'd think . . .'

'Lin,' he interrupted abruptly.

'No, David,' she said whitely and put her coffee cup down with suddenly shaking hands, 'please let's not start on all that again. Even hardened sinners like myself need a break . . .' She stopped abruptly and bit her lip. 'Look,' she said very quietly, 'I'm fine. By tomorrow I'll be back to normal.' She lay back feeling exhausted and wished he would go away so that she could go to sleep again. Sleep, she thought, that seems to be my only salvation at the moment.

'Tomorrow,' he said slowly, 'I'm flying up to Karendale for a week. I'd like you to come with me—if you feel up to it. If not we could delay it for a day.'

Lineesa lifted her head and stared at him incredulously. Karendale was a cattle station in Queensland in which David and Bronwen had shares with several cousins of the family.

'Have you ever been to that part of the world, South-Western Queensland?' he asked.

'I . . . no,' Lineesa said dazedly. 'But . . .'

'It can be very beautiful,' he said quietly. 'Especially now. They had good winter rains which means the wild flowers will be out. It's . . .' he hesitated, 'people think of it as desert country and it's certainly flat and often arid but there is water there in great artesian basins so stock can survive there by means of bore water. And in a good season like this one promises to be, there are grasslands as well as the wild flowers, there are forests of cypress pine, claypans full of water and the coolibahs beside them full of bird-life. Have you ever seen a coolibah tree? And the bird-life is incredible. Pelicans, pink and white Major Mitchell cockatoos, emus and of course wild life too, like kangaroos. It's,' he hesitated again and looked wry, 'one of my favourite parts of the world at this time of the year. Although to many, the term "Heartbreak Corner" is more apt.'

'To Burke and Wills it was,' she said involuntarily and was surprised at herself.

'Yes,' he agreed. 'Yet certain tribes of Aborigines managed to survive in the area for between thirty to fifty thousand years. In fact Karendale is named after one such tribe—the Karendala. They ... understood the delicate balance of nature, I guess, because it *can* be an incredibly hostile environment. It's an area of flood and drought—I've seen the channel country, "the overflow" as they call it, between the Diamantina River and Cooper Creek, when it's like a solid sheet of water for miles and miles and this happens regularly. I've also seen droughts but it's an area that has remarkable powers of recuperation—provided the balance of nature is not too drastically interfered with.'

'You mean over-grazing and over-stocking,' she said.

He raised his eyebrows fleetingly.

'Oh, geography was one of my major subjects at school,' she said. 'I was also fascinated by those early, epic explorers like Sturt, who first discovered Cooper Creek, and the ill-fated Burke and Wills, who died beside it, but that was over the border, wasn't it? Near Innamincka?'

'My dear, Lin,' he said after a moment with his lips twitching, 'remind me to think twice before I allow myself to sound like a school teacher again in your company.'

'No,' she smiled faintly. 'You sounded as if you really ... cared.' Then she sobered and moved self-consciously and looked away.

'Would you like to see it in the flesh, so to speak? If you've read so much about it ...'

'David . . .'

'If you're also a fan of Australian poetry,' he interrupted and reached over to pick up a slim volume of verse from her bedside table, 'it's *Clancy of the Overflow* country.'

She held her breath as he leafed through the book but nothing fluttered out and she breathed again when he laid it on the bed open to the Banjo Patterson poem. She stared at the book, then lifted her eyes to his.

'David—why are you doing this?' she whispered.

'Because I think you need to get away,' he said levelly. 'Trevor thinks so too.'

'That's,' she said with an effort, 'surely above and beyond the kind of concern you need to feel for me, though?'

'Is it?' he said pensively.

'Well, yes. It's like . . . it's like—I can't understand it. Wouldn't it be better just to send me away somewhere for a week?'

'Better for who?'

'For both of us, I should think.'

He frowned faintly. Then he said, 'Lin, I never meant to harm your health. Nor did I realise until last night . . . that I was.'

'There's . . . I keep saying this, but there's nothing wrong with me.'

'If you have a nervous breakdown, there will be,' he said drily.

'I thought . . . I thought it might be something like that,' she said dazedly and licked her lips. 'You want me to be of sound mind and fighting fit when I finally give in and confess I'm everything you think I am. Is that it? Are you afraid that if I'm not, you'll find yourself feeling a little sorry for me, that you'll not be able to hate me as much as you'd like to—as you have?'

He smiled, a cool, chiselled movement of his lips that didn't reach his eyes. 'Perhaps,' he said. 'But I think that's happened already, you see. I find that words like hate and revenge, don't spring to mind so easily when I think of you these days.' His blue eyes travelled over her sombrely. 'No. I find now that I really want to get to the bottom of you, Lin, because in some ways you've surprised me and puzzled me. And in some ways you've proved me wrong. I don't think anyone who was as desperately distraught as you were last night, could be quite the shallow ... person I took you for. So I'm offering a—truce. Will you accept the offer?'

She stared at him with parted lips and stunned eyes. 'And what,' she managed to say finally, 'happens when you ... get to the bottom of me?'

'We'll call it quits ...'

'You mean, you'll let me go? You won't ... my mother ...'

'The title deeds to your mother's house will go into your name, Lin.' He stood up abruptly.

'Wouldn't it ... be simpler just to let me go now?' she whispered.

'Maybe,' he conceded. 'But then I could be spending the rest of my life wondering about you—and concerned,' he said. 'And you ... well, let's just say this is a better way to do it, I think. Shall we leave tomorrow or Tuesday?'

'I ... it ... I ...' she said helplessly and found she couldn't go on.

'Tomorrow then,' he said and smiled briefly. 'So that we don't have time to change our minds. I'll send Mrs Livingstone up to you ...'

Lineesa stared up at the ceiling and wondered

vaguely at the number of times she'd done this recently. It's becoming a habit, she thought. Sleeping, and staring at nothing. I know this ceiling off by heart . . .

She looked away, around the apricot bedroom. It was tidy and the sherbet-green armchair that David had drawn up beside the bed, was restored to its position beside the fireplace.

She was herself restored, too. Mrs Livingstone had seen to that. She'd drawn a bath and heaped into it some jade-green bath crystals, and murmured that Mrs Marchmont would feel much better after soaking in the warm water.

'Mrs Marchmont—the last one that is—always used to say this bath was worth its weight in gold,' she'd added. 'She should have known, she spent enough time in it.'

'Oh?' Lineesa had stirred the green water absently with her hand. 'Did you . . . no, it doesn't matter.'

'Did I what,' Mrs Livingstone had persisted.

'I . . . spoke without thinking,' Lineesa had replied.

But although that had appeared to satisfy Mrs Livingstone, it hadn't been quite true. David's parents had been dead for a number of years apparently and apart from Mr Livingstone, who took care of the garden and the horses, no-one at Marchmont made much mention of them. But in those infrequent references when they applied to the last Mrs Marchmont, there was a curious undertone that Lineesa seemed to catch. A sort of reservation which made her think of Piers' comment about his mother. But when Piers had said that, she hadn't been quite sure if he'd been serious. And Mr Livingstone, who spoke frequently and affectionately of the late Mr Marchmont,

senior, never ever mentioned the late *Mrs*
Marchmont, senior . . .

Not that it's any of my business anyway,
Lineesa thought to herself as she lay in the big bed
and found that her earlier desire to sleep had quite
deserted her.

She moved and pleated the white satin sheet
with her fingers. The bed had been re-made with
fresh sheets and she wore a fresh white nightgown
with tiny puff sleeves and a lacy bodice and her
hair, which Mrs Livingstone had brushed, shone
dark gold in the soft light of the bedside lamp as it
fell over her shoulders.

If I didn't imagine what David said in this very
room not long ago, she went on to think, not
anything to do with any of the Marchmonts will
be my business any more. I'll be free . . . Yet, what
he's suggested seems like a kind of test—or am I
imagining *that*?

She sighed and laid her head back and reflected
with a certain wryness that while she should be
filled with elation, she was in fact possessed by a
sense of nervous apprehension. 'Because I have the
feeling he's not going to like what he finds even if
he does get to the bottom of me?' she murmured.
'But why should I *care*? I've suffered enough at the
hands of David Marchmont, you'd think, wouldn't
you?'

But the ceiling to which this query had been
addressed, predictably vouchsafed no answer and
she grimaced and reached over to turn off the
lamp.

Instead though, she picked up the book of verse
that was still on the bedside table. And she held it
by its spine so that the pages fluttered open and a
slip of paper fell out. It was the only one, which
might have been why it had escaped detection, but

as she glanced at it, she felt her nerves tighten as she thought of David reading it. In fact the thought of David reading any of her work was bad enough, but especially this one.

'How can you explain a hatred that isn't always that?' she read silently.

'How can you put it into words that don't sound trite?
How can you put it into words at all
When its like some dark, hidden depth to your soul . . .'

She closed her eyes and crumpled the slip of paper in her palm. Deep stuff, she thought. Not quite my usual style. I wonder what David would think if he knew I was a budding poet? That if nothing else this marriage has achieved for me, it has inspired me to write verse for which, some of it, I've even been paid? Not that one could make a living out of it precisely. And not that this marriage has actually inspired me, but rather the state of mind it's induced in me has made me grasp at any avenue of . . . mental escape.

She thought of some of the poems she'd had published under her maiden name of Creighton. Descriptive ones of the countryside, a couple of funny verses for children and one bitter, satirical piece about nuclear arms.

She'd also had a short story accepted for publication in a magazine that had not so far appeared in print.

Maybe I can pursue writing or journalism as a career when I'm . . . discarded from this marriage, she mused. Perhaps I should take a notebook and pencil to the Diamantina and Cooper Creek? After all it's a fantastic opportunity which might not come my way again.

And maybe ... no, why should I be able to write love poems? What do I know about love? I only know about hate and—guilt, and who wants to write about that? Living it is bad enough ...

She stared bleakly at the book on the bed and then opened her palm and smoothed out the crumpled bit of paper and slid it back between the pages.

'One day,' she whispered, 'I might be able to finish that—for once and for all, finish it. And then I'll destroy it ...'

CHAPTER FOUR

'THERE,' Mrs Livingstone said the next morning. 'I've packed mostly jeans and shorts and a couple of thick jumpers. It can get cold up there at night.'

'Then you've been to Karendale, Mrs Livingstone?' Lineesa said.

'I have,' Mrs Livingstone answered somewhat drily.

Lineesa looked up and grinned faintly. 'You don't sound as if it's *your* favourite part of the world.'

'True, it's not. I'm not a great one for nature in the raw. Marchmont is about as far from civilisation that I care to be,' Mrs Livingstone said with a grimace. 'It's bush, ma'am, let me warn you! And as for the flies ... But there, Mr David loves it, always has since he was a boy. He spent a whole year up there once ... But it is a man's world and I feel sorry for the women who have to live up there. In fact, I really can't understand why he couldn't have chosen somewhere else to take you for your little holiday. Now, are you sure you're feeling all right?' Her bright, dark eyes searched Lineesa's face anxiously.

Lineesa returned her look warmly. 'Quite sure,' she murmured. 'You mustn't worry about me.'

'Well I do.' Mrs Livingstone looked faintly belligerent for a moment, then she laughed and with a tinge of embarrassment and turned away to check her immaculate packing.

It's a funny thing, Lineesa reflected. If anyone should dislike and distrust me, Mrs Livingstone should. She, more than anyone else, must realise this is a strange marriage. And since she's been at Marchmont for twenty-five years or thereabouts, and since she's patently fond of David, you'd think *I'd* be her least favourite person. But after those first few moments of being the very correct housekeeper, we're now . . . friends of a kind.

'Well they do say a change is as good as a holiday,' Mrs Livingstone said brightly then, and straightened up. 'There . . . That's everything I can think of. And don't worry, I'll ring Mrs Creighton for you every day, just like you do.'

Lineesa frowned. She'd rung her mother that morning and told her she was going away. Her mother had not minded in the least. In fact it was Lineesa who minded—worried rather. And wondered often if she shouldn't get someone in to look after her mother, a live-in companion. I will do it when I came back, she vowed. And thought almost immediately, but there'll be no need, will there? I'll be able to live with her . . .

'There's Mr David coming for you now,' Mrs Livingstone said, and Lineesa tensed for those words seemed to have a prophetic, eerie quality and she looked up as David strolled into the bedroom, and she didn't know that her hazel eyes were wide and tinged with a faint wariness as she looked at him.

But if he noticed, he didn't comment on it, merely said, 'Are you ready, Lin?'

'. . . Yes.'

A day later David said, *'Hell,'* and changed gear viciously. The large Land-Rover they were in surged forward drunkenly with a peculiar grating noise and he swore again and braked so that they came to a juddering halt.

Lineesa looked at him questioningly.

'Another flat tyre,' he said scathingly, and added impatiently, 'I'm beginning to think I'm bloody well jinxed!'

'Well, it wasn't your fault that something went wrong with the plane,' she said.

'No, but it was my fault for not waiting at Windorah for it to be repaired,' he said savagely. 'It was my decision to hire a Land-Rover and drive to Karendale.'

'But . . .'

'Dear Lin, don't try to appease me,' he shot at her. 'I *know* this bloody country. I know this is always on the cards. It could take us all bloody day to get there!'

'But we might have had to wait in Windorah for two or three days before the part for the plane was flown in,' she said mildly.

'Well at least there's a pub there, and a bed for you,' he said moodily.

'David,' she said, 'perhaps I shouldn't say this, seeing I don't have to change the tyres, but I'd far rather be doing this than sitting in the pub at Windorah. And I slept like a top last night so I'm in no need of a bed for a good few hours yet. You don't have to think of me as an invalid, you know.'

He shrugged and then grinned at her. 'Sorry,' he said. 'All right, hop out and sit on the shady side of the Land-Rover and I'll change the . . . tyre.'

Lineesa smiled inwardly. 'Can I help?'

'No. Just do as you're told.'

She did and took a deep breath of air that smelt and tasted somehow different, and looked around her. They were temporarily stranded on a vast plain that stretched to the horizon all around and was a sea of green, fresh grass dotted with cotton-bush, salt-bush and blue-bush scrub. At least that is what David had told her it was. They'd left Windorah early in the morning after a night spent in twin beds and a minimum amount of embarrassment for her, seeing as David had been out on the airfield until long after she'd fallen asleep, and had risen before she had.

And when he'd suggested driving to Karendale— a drive that took four to five hours normally, she'd been quite happy to comply because the early morning had had a fresh dewy beauty to it that was quite intoxicating. He'd then produced a hired Land-Rover, already loaded with the stuff they'd arranged to pick up at Windorah late the previous afternoon.

That's when David's troubles had started, mercifully, otherwise they could have found themselves mid-air with a faulty engine. But up until then, the flight from Sydney had been near perfect—a new experience for Lineesa who had previously only flown in a commercial jet-liner. David had piloted the light plane himself and appeared as competent and at ease at it as if it was a car. And by design she'd suspected, they'd landed at Tamworth in the New England area of New South Wales and driven into town for morning tea, and again at Toowoomba on the Darling Downs of Queensland, for a late lunch. So she'd not only experienced the magic of flying in a light plane from which one could see the changing pageant of the scenery below, but seen some of two provincial centres as well.

And in the process, curiously, had felt herself relaxing more than she'd dreamt possible, as the day had progressed.

Mrs Livingstone was right, she mused as she waved away the hundreds of little black flies. A change must be as good as a holiday—and the flies are dreadful!

But she smiled as she thought this, and looked around a little disbelievingly. To be sitting, not far as distances go, in this part of the world, from Cooper Creek which had the distinction of having two major rivers as its tributaries, the Thompson and the Barcoo, and the added distinction of flowing inland to Lake Eyre in South Australia, although once over the border it was more of a series of swamps and waterholes—is quite incredible! She reflected. I didn't really ever imagine when I was so fascinated by Sturt's account of his travels in this area, and Augustus Gregory's—I'm sure he actually passed through what is now Windorah—that one day I'd be here myself . . .

But she shivered suddenly then as she remembered some of the incredible hardships those early explorers had suffered, and remembered those who'd never returned, and she felt suddenly the vastness and the implacability of the ancient landscape all around her even though it was decked now in summer finery, and she thought of David's description of miles and miles of water and then pitiless drought . . . And she jumped as he came round the side of the Land-Rover and said, 'Right, let's try again!'

'Oh!' She went a little pink as he raised his eyebrows. 'You . . . I was lost in thought,' she said wryly. 'You startled me.'

'A penny for them,' he said and put out a hand to help her to her feet.

She grimaced. 'Well, history—and how I wouldn't like to have to depend on this part of a world for a livelihood. I think, as an individual, you'd feel so insignificant . . . at least that's how I was feeling a moment ago.'

'Sorry you came?'

She looked up into his eyes and said hastily, 'Oh no! I wouldn't have missed this for the world ...' She tailed off and bit her lip, feeling suddenly awkward—as if she shouldn't be expressing sentiments like that.

But he smiled slightly and murmured, 'I'm glad.'

Lineesa stared at him for a moment and experienced a curious sensation. She became aware of her heart beat, as if it had tripped and was now racing. Because he smiled at me? she wondered and turned away just a little clumsily. Well, it's not a frequent occurrence, is it? I mean, not genuinely. But then since we left Marchmont, this has been a different David, hasn't it? Perhaps that's why I feel so different ...

'There's a house over there,' she said about half an hour later. Since leaving the beef road which connected Windorah and Birdsville, and the dirt road, if it could be called that, that had produced their two flat tyres, they were now on a barely discernible track.

'Yes,' David said absently. 'It's the Mullers. We're on their property. It adjoins Karendale. We'll stop and say good-day. I haven't seen Fred Muller for ... over twelve months I guess. They've had a few bad years. I wouldn't have been surprised if they'd pulled up and left. I'll just check they're home.'

Lineesa watched him mount the front steps of the dilapidated old house and then looked round at the unlovely yard. It was really only an area of beaten earth that surrounded the house and it was littered with junk, old tyres, a rusting, old-fashioned kerosene refrigerator ...

She realised then her name was being called urgently and she jerked her head back to see

David beckoning her from the verandah.

'There's trouble here,' he said grimly. 'Fred and his wife are . . . well, see for yourself.'

She saw as soon as she stepped into what appeared to be a sitting room cum kitchen cum bedroom. A man lay motionless on the floor and beside him was a woman who was moaning slightly and retching.

'Oh . . .' Lineesa went down on her knees beside the woman while David knelt beside the man and put his ear to his chest.

'Is he . . .?'

'He's alive,' David said and lifted the man's eyelids. 'He seems to be in some sort of a coma.'

The woman moaned then and moved and said something unintelligible.

'What is it?' Lineesa said clearly but the woman slumped back and sweat beaded the pale, greeny-grey skin of her face. Lineesa lifted her eyes to David's.

'I don't know what's wrong,' he said. 'But for them both to be like this . . . it could be food poisoning. In which case we need to get cracking.'

'How?'

'They must have a radio. I can get a helicopter sent from—somewhere.'

The Mullers did have a radio, they discovered, on the enclosed back porch but it didn't appear to be working.

David's face tightened with exasperation as he fiddled with it.

'Do you know anything about radios?' Lineesa asked shakenly.

'Yes. Whether I can do anything with this ancient model remains to be seen,' he said harshly.

'Well, I'll go and see if I can help them,' she said and turned away.

'Good girl,' he answered briefly.

But there was little enough she could do for Fred Muller and his wife other than bathe their faces with water she found in a can beside the sink. The room was sparsely furnished—in fact it was heart-rendingly bare. A large double mattress on the floor, two sagging couches and a kitchen table and chairs and two cupboards beside the sink, and an enormous, old-fashioned wood burning stove. But the place was clean and neat and there was a bunch of wild flowers in a jam jar on the table. Lineesa looked down at the woman who now seemed to have relapsed into a similar coma as her husband, and her heart went out to her. To have to live in this kind of isolation with so little . . .

'I think we're right,' David said, appearing suddenly beside her. 'It seems to work intermittently now—there could be a lot of sunspot activity causing interference—but I got on to a surveying company's helicopter frequency quite by chance, and the pilot seems to have a fair idea of the area, he was on his way to Windorah.'

'Thank God,' she said. 'I don't like the look of them. Wasn't it lucky we passed by though? You see, you weren't jinxed after all!'

He grinned. 'No.'

Fifteen minutes later the helicopter settled into the yard, and the pilot and his passenger, with David's aid, loaded the inert bodies of Fred Muller and his wife aboard. The pilot, who said he had some first aid training, agreed that it looked like food poisoning.

'Probably living off the smell of an oil rag, poor devils,' he said with a comprehensive look around. 'They might have taken a chance with some old, tinned food . . .'

Lineesa felt tears prick her eyelids. Now I've

really experienced Heartbreak Corner, she thought.

They watched the helicopter lift off clumsily and then fly like a bird until it was only a dot in the sky.

'Well,' David said with a glance at his watch. 'We better hit the track, Mrs Marchmont. I told you it might take us all day to make Karendale.'

'How much further?'

'Oh—a couple of hours, before dark anyway. I'll just check the shed,' he waved to a building behind the house that looked as if one good puff of wind would blow it down. 'They might have some livestock. Won't be long.'

Lineesa started to walk towards the Land-Rover but she'd only taken a few steps when she stopped and frowned and swung round. She could have sworn she'd heard a faint cry but as she stood and listened there was only silence. Perhaps it was a bird, she thought. But then it came again and from the direction of the house. Perhaps they've got a bird, in a cage, but I didn't see one . . .'

Then the cry came yet again as she mounted the front steps and she thought, that isn't a bird! But there was no sign of life in the room that could be truly called a living room, and for the first time she noticed a door that didn't lead to the back verandah and she ran across to it and flung it open, expecting to see she knew not what, but least of all what she did see.

It was a small room with only a single narrow bed in it and a small chest of drawers that was missing one drawer, because that drawer was on the bed. And in the drawer was a tiny baby nestled into a pillow and as she gazed at it spellbound, it waved its fists and opened its mouth and began to cry in earnest.

'Oh darling!' she breathed and picked it up. 'Oh honey, we didn't even know about you. Oh God! Thank heavens you woke up!'

But the infant appeared not to be interested in what might have been its fate. Instead, it stopped crying at the sound of Lineesa's voice and the feel of her arms and turned its downy little head to her breasts with urgent sucking movements of its rosebud mouth.

'Oh dear,' Lineesa whispered. 'No, sweetheart, I'm afraid I can't help you . . .' She broke off at a sound and looked up to see David standing in the doorway with an arrested look on his face.

'Christ,' he said at last. 'I didn't know they had any kids!'

'I don't think they've had this one for long,' she said. 'It's very little.' She held the baby out for his inspection.

He eyed it. 'It is that. How old do you think it is? I haven't had much experience of babies—other than Bronwen's and I don't have much to do with them until they start to walk and talk.' He grimaced faintly.

She hesitated. 'I haven't had much experience either except by . . . correspondence course you could say.'

He raised his eyebrows. 'What do you mean?'

'Well, I did a mothercraft course at school. It was compulsory but we didn't ever have the real thing to work on . . . I'd say not more than two months probably. And very hungry,' she added as the baby began to cry again. 'Which could be a bit of a problem! There, there, honey,' she crooned and cuddled the baby again, only to have it do exactly as it had done before with a heart-breaking eagerness.

She lifted her eyes to David's and felt a faint

heat come to her cheeks at the wryly amused look she saw in them. 'See what I mean?' she said a little defiantly.

'Yes, I do,' he murmured. 'A problem indeed. But there could be . . .'

'A bottle!' She said the word at the same time he did. 'Of course . . . at least I hope so. And something to put in it.'

'Right. Let's look. Is there nothing you can do to stop it crying in the meantime?' he queried with a faint smile.

'I'll change it. It's also very wet. That might help. If you'd like to start looking . . .'

'Yes, ma'am,' he said, and left her.

But a dry nappy did not appease the baby for very long, nor did there appear to be anything resembling an infant's feeding bottle on the premises.

'Well, we'll just have to put up with it crying until we get to Karendale,' David said at last.

'Her . . .' Lineesa said.

'Her then. Not that there are any babies there to my knowledge but there are two families on the property and several children.'

'The motion of the Land-Rover might sooth her, you never know,' Lineesa said.

He threw her a glinting look. 'I don't think you could call the motion we're about to encounter anything but bone-jarring.'

'Oh . . .'

He laughed at her expression. 'Never mind,' he said. 'I've got strong nerves . . . I think. Let's get going before it's too late.'

'Too late?'

'Well, I'd rather not be driving in the dark. It's not that easy in the daylight . . . Bring all its gear.'

But inexplicably, when they were loaded in to the Land-Rover, baby and all, it wouldn't start.

And for the life of her, Lineesa couldn't help laughing a little at the look on his face.

'My dear Lin,' he said bitterly, 'the next time you're tempted to tell me I'm not jinxed, will you kindly shut up! You do realise what this means, don't you? We're stuck here for the night with a squalling infant, a possibly faulty radio . . . *hell*!'

She sobered and apologised.

'That's all very well,' he said. 'But so far as I can see the only other form of transport on the place is a motorbike. Now that means I can go for help on it and leave you two here alone . . .'

She tensed visibly.

'I thought not,' he said. 'Or we can spend the night and I can try to repair this . . .' He hit the steering wheel with the flat of his hand.

'The radio?' she hazarded. 'Maybe . . .'

'Maybe, but I doubt it. I suspect I got on to that chopper with its dying gasp. Which means, you'll have to bend your mind to the problem of feeding *it*.' He gestured to the baby.

'Her . . . Well,' she thought for a moment. 'I saw it done in a movie once with a glove. They pricked holes in the fingertips. Was there any powdered milk in the house?'

'No. But I'd be a bit wary of any of the foodstuffs in the house anyway . . . Hang on.' He turned towards the back of the Land Rover. 'Those supplies we picked up Windorah. Let's see what we've got.'

Ten minutes later, Lineesa was back in the house with a precious tin of powdered milk in one hand and the baby under her arm and David was detaching one of the portable water containers from the Land-Rover.

'Best if we use our own water too,' he'd said. 'There could be something in their water tanks for all we know. And best if we boiled it. We'll have to light the stove . . .'

'Not long now, sweetheart,' she said to the baby as she put it back into its improvised cot. 'I don't know about the glove idea. It might only work in the movies and we might not *have* a glove but at least we can try with a teaspoon—or something! I'll just put your things away. Oh!' She'd pulled open a drawer as she'd spoken and it had come right out of the chest to reveal an object that must have been right at the back of it—a brand new baby's bottle complete with teat, all still in a cellophane wrapper. 'Eureka!' she cried and frightened the tiny girl on the bed into temporary silence and also brought David to the door in a hurry.

She held the bottle up with a flourish. 'Our troubles are over! Or,' she looked at him with a sudden wariness, 'perhaps I shouldn't say that— just yet?'

'I was premature,' Lineesa said a couple of hours later with a sigh. It was getting dark outside and cold but the bare main room of the Muller's house was at least warm and almost cheery in the reflected firelight from the stove and the light of one hurricane lamp. She and David were sitting at the table and had just finished a meal concocted from the fresh tinned foods bound for Karendale. Lineesa had eaten awkwardly with the baby cradled in one arm because whenever she attempted to put it down, it started to cry.

'What's the problem?' David said. He looked weary and dirty. He'd spent the remaining hours of daylight alternately trying to fix the Land-

Rover and the radio—the radio at least, with no success.

'She hates the bottle. She coughs and splutters and pulls terrible faces and I don't think she has any idea what to do with the teat once it's in her mouth.'

'Why? I mean . . .'

'She's just not used to it, I guess,' Lineesa said tiredly. 'But we'll persevere, won't we, poppet,' she murmured and kissed the top of the baby's head softly.

And when she looked up it was to find David staring at her sombrely. 'What . . . is it?' she said uncertainly.

He blinked and shrugged. 'Oh, nothing. You've been terrific today. Anyone else would have probably been cursing me left, right and centre for landing them in a mess like this.'

And although Lineesa knew she had a long, tiring night ahead of her, for so far the baby had only been persuaded to consume about a quarter of a bottle, she felt a sudden warm glow within and she smiled and said gruffly, 'Thanks.'

'Bloody rain!' David said savagely the next afternoon. 'It never bloody rains but it pours in this God-forsaken part of the world. It shouldn't *be* raining at this time of the year.'

Lineesa looked at him. Daylight that morning had brought them the vista of heavy, swollen clouds low overhead and steady rain. And contrary to David's expressed expectation that it would pass over pretty quickly, but that they'd wait until it did and then set off in the repaired Land-Rover—it had just kept raining.

'Well, we might be . . . marooned,' she said, 'but we're not in danger, are we? I mean we've got supplies and . . .'

'I really had no idea you were such an eternal optimist, Lin,' he said impatiently. 'No-one knows where we are ... If the baby's parents have regained consciousness, they'll be frantic! If ... what the hell are you doing now?'

Lineesa looked at the big tin bowl of warm water she'd put on the table and the towel she'd laid beside it, and then at the baby lying contentedly in its drawer, staring fixedly at the hurricane lamp that hung from the ceiling.

'I'm going to give her a bath,' she said mildly. 'Don't worry, I didn't use any of our water. I just put out every container I could lay my hands on, to catch the rain water. Come on, little love,' she said to the baby and lifted her up gently and laid her on the towel. 'You'll like this ...'

'I gather she's taking more kindly to the bottle now,' David said drily. 'She hasn't cried for ages.'

'Yes, she is,' Lineesa said serenely. 'I think hunger got the upper hand. Not that she's exactly ecstatic about it, but she took nearly six ounces and slept for nearly three hours. There.' She lowered the little body into the water. 'You'll like this ...' she said again.

Like was a mild word for the delight one very small baby girl managed to express. She kicked her tiny feet and made soft cooing noises as Lineesa splashed the water over her tummy. Lineesa laughed and looked up to see that even David was smiling reluctantly.

Then he said abruptly, 'You're enjoying this, aren't you, Lin?' He gestured to the baby and around the room.

'I ...' She stopped and bit her lip and looked guilty. 'I shouldn't be. People will be concerned as you say ...'

'But you are.'

'Yes,' she said very quietly and lifted the baby out and wrapped her in the towel. 'I . . . well it's different I suppose.'

'You . . .' he hesitated, 'you're looking better.'

She grimaced. 'I didn't realise I was looking sick. I *wasn't* sick.'

'No. But you were looking—strained and haunted. And as if your nerves were very close to the surface.'

Lineesa didn't comment immediately. Instead she concentrated on drying the baby thoroughly and started to dress her. Then she said, 'Mrs Livingstone said that a change is as good as a holiday. Well, honeybunch? How does that feel? I wish I knew what your name was—I might have to invent one for you. You're so pretty! I hope they called you after a flower or something nice.'

'A desert rose,' David said, and she turned to find him standing right beside her looking down at the peaceful infant. 'Poor kid,' he added. 'She hasn't got much to look forward to.'

'She might have a lot of love to look forward to,' Lineesa said. 'I think she's been well cared for. Look at those fat little cheeks.'

'Love doesn't pay the bills.'

'I know, but it helps. Is there nothing anyone can do for the Mullers?'

'He's a proud man,' David said. 'I offered once. Well, I offered to buy his run and let him stay on to manage it. But he refused although he lost a lot of cattle in the last drought.' He shrugged.

'They might accept an offer now,' Lineesa said thoughtfully. 'With a baby . . . I just hope they're alive,' she added intensely.

He put a hand on her shoulder and pressed it. 'Look,' he said after moment. 'Your little rose has fallen asleep.'

The baby only woke twice during the night and each time took its bottle without any fuss. But after the second feeding, Lineesa found sleep eluding her, and she realised she was cold for one thing. Mainly, she realised too, because the fire in the stove was nearly out. And she took off the heavy jumper she'd added to a fleecy-lined tracksuit she'd donned for the night, and tucked it over the baby in its drawer.

She and the drawer were occupying the double mattress while David was asleep on the single mattress they'd taken from the bed in the baby's room. But blankets were as scarce in this house as most other commodities. And the rain was still drumming on the roof eerily and she thought fleetingly of miles and miles of water, and Burke and Wills who had perished beside Cooper Creek—I'm virtually in the heart of Australia, there's no-one for *miles* and miles a—I'm being fanciful, she chided herself. And rose stealthily.

She stoked the fire and added some wood and it flamed satisfactorily and cast flickering orange shadows on the wall. Fire, she thought, and set a pan of water on top of the stove, has to be man's greatest comforter!

And when the water boiled, she made herself a cup of instant coffee, added more wood to the stove, and retreated to the double mattress with her cup which she set down on the floor, and leant back against the wall.

Then the baby stirred and she stroked the little mound it made beneath its coverings and her jumper, and when it settled she reached for her cup and looked across at David. He was awake with his head resting on one arm and his eyes resting on her.

Their glances caught and held.

'Don't tell me,' he said very quietly after a moment. 'You're thinking of Burke and Wills again?'

'. . . How did you know?' she whispered.

'Something in your eyes.'

'I . . . was cold. Would you like a cup of coffee?'

'Yes. I'll get it.'

He came back to his mattress a few minutes later and pushed it with his foot until it adjoined the double one.

'The closer we are, the warmer we'll be,' he said and sat down like she had, with his back to the wall, and so that only the drawer's width with the baby in it, separated them.

And apart from the rain on the roof, it was quiet and it grew warmer and the firelight flickered through the open front of the stove.

'People . . . will be looking for us by now, won't they,' she said.

He grimaced and sipped his coffee. 'Until this rain lifts, there's not much they can do. The cloud's so low, it could be suicidal to fly and the channels will be rising, so . . . But from our point of view, you and I, they won't be too concerned yet.'

'Oh?'

'No.' He smiled wryly. 'You might not believe this, but I have a fair reputation for being an accomplished bushman.'

'But I think you've done very well!' She returned his smile. 'I mean it wasn't *your* fault . . .' She stopped, and her smile broadened. 'All right, I won't say it. But you did fix the Land-Rover and . . .'

'I also made one glaring error,' he interrupted. 'I shouldn't have left Windorah without a radio. I can't get a peep out of that one now.' He gestured

—to the back veranda where he'd spent most of the day fiddling with the Muller's radio.

'All the same,' she said quietly. 'I feel ... safe with you somehow.' She looked across at him with a tinge of surprise in her hazel eyes. But it was true, she realised.

His mouth twisted. 'That surprises you obviously,' he said drily. 'I don't blame you ...'

'No ...'

'It should. I've not only landed you in this mess but at times I've exhibited enough—hostility, towards you to make you feel quite the opposite, possibly,' he said ironically.

She hesitated. 'I think,' she said at last, 'it's come more as a surprise to find that you are— well, we live ... *lived* such a different life in Sydney, I had no idea this, the bush and the outback—appealed to you so much.'

'Nor I you,' he said after a long pause.

She sipped her coffee. Then the baby murmured and she put her hand on it and stroked it again and it settled once more and David watched her hand, slender and tanned with its plain gold wedding ring, and he lifted his eyes to her at last.

'Tell me about Piers, Lin,' he said.

She flinched and looked away.

'Lin?' His voice was very quiet but there was an underlying determination to it that was impossible to misread.

She took a breath and blinked away the sudden shimmer of tears that had come to her eyes.

'All right,' she said huskily. And she told him— told him what she'd said to Piers that first night, told him about the day he'd taken her to the races and introduced her to everyone as the Queen's cousin ... all the little things about their relationship, which had been the essence of it for

her. 'It,' she hesitated, 'to me it was more like a
boy girl kind of thing. We had a lot of fun, as if we
were still silly teenagers . . .'

'And that satisfied you?' he queried.

She shrugged after a moment. 'Yes it did. I
hadn't felt like a teenager for a long time, although
I was barely more than one, technically.'

'And you never—thought that Piers might be
after . . . more?'

Lineesa closed her eyes. And after a long pause,
she whispered, 'Yes. In my heart of hearts I knew.
But he made it so easy for me to—pretend that it
wasn't anything more, I . . . let things slide along.
You see, I really *liked* him too. I mean, I grew
terribly fond of him. And sometimes, I even
wondered if it would be . . . all right to be married
or whatever, to someone I liked so much. But that
night, when he asked me to marry him, I knew I
couldn't do that to him. It wasn't fair. And I knew
too, how unfair to him I'd been by letting things
get that far, by burying my head in the sand like
an ostrich and refusing to admit what I knew was
happening to him.' She looked up suddenly and
her eyes were bleak and full of a terrible, hurting,
self mockery. 'I did that to the only man I'd met
who thought more of getting to know me than
taking me to bed. Oh, I told myself I couldn't be
responsible for every man who was attracted to
me. I told myself I wasn't to blame for a certain
arrangement of features and limbs—after all I'd
only inherited those genes. And I told myself that
I'd never . . . been deliberately sexy with Piers. I
mean the most we ever did was hold hands a
couple of times and I think he kissed me three
times but only in fun . . .'

'So you never slept with him?' David interrupted.

Lineesa winced and wondered why. I always knew what kind of person he thought I was . . .

'No,' she said with difficulty. 'But that's no defence. Neither are any of the other things I told myself. You can't walk through life claiming no responsibility, particularly not in regard to people you like and *value*. And so far as being sexy goes, it is . . . it was my trade. So in effect, the damage was done before I ever met Piers, done cold-bloodedly too, and for money. Which I made a fair amount of in the course of my career. That's why I took up modelling in the first place. And that's why I should be the last person to quibble about the . . . repercussions, to me personally.'

The fire crackled and the rain beat steadily on the roof. But there was no other sound in the house. Lineesa was plucking the wool of her jumper that covered the baby but quite unaware that she was doing it. And she was staring down at the coffee cup in her other hand, unseeingly.

He said at last, 'Is that what you meant when you said, if only I knew how right your mother had been?'

'Did I say that?' Her voice cracked a little.

He nodded.

'Well, my mother was horrified at first. She thought it was unladylike. At the time *I* thought she was being desperately old-fashioned. "Unlady-like" is a term that doesn't seem to mean much these days. But I think now that she was right . . .'

'You're very bitter, Lin,' he said quietly. 'Leaving Piers out of it and what's—happened since . . .'

'Yes I am,' she said huskily. 'Bitter and often disgusted with myself not to have known better. They say sex sells the world—they're right, otherwise they wouldn't have used me to sell cars, used me in a bikini to sell a brand of wine. But nobody forced me into it. I went along willingly with this wholesale commercialisation of something ... something—I can't explain it. All I can say is that if I've been made to feel cheap and easy and least of all a lady, I can't blame anyone but myself. Nor,' she added barely audibly, 'can I forgive myself for what happened to Piers on account of it. You see you can't separate ... you said a moment ago, leaving Piers aside ... But you can't do that because what happened was a direct consequence of it all. If he hadn't treated me like a—like a *person* instead of ...' She stopped and shrugged, and found herself battling with a fresh set of tears. 'The last person on earth I wanted to hurt was Piers,' she whispered.

He watched her for a long time. Then he said, 'You're wrong about one thing, Lin. Whatever you may have done differently, short of becoming a nun, you'd always have attracted men, you always will. You have that kind of beauty ... you're even beautiful now, when you're crying.' He smiled slightly as her eyes, fringed by wet lashes sticking together in clumps, widened. 'But it isn't only your face and figure. It's the way you move too, it's your hands, it's a delicacy and grace about you—an infinite femininity. But it's *not* your fault, you're wrong about that. And no beautiful woman should have to carry it like a cross because the only thing wrong about it, comes when they use it wrongly. The fact that no man alive could look at you and not ... entertain certain thoughts about you, is just human nature.'

She stiffened and he saw it and his lips twisted. 'Oh yes,' he said drily, 'I know I claimed immunity to you once, but that wasn't quite true.'

Her lips parted and her eyes were stunned.

Irresistible!

4 FREE NOVELS AND A SURPRISE GIFT

DELIVERED RIGHT TO YOUR HOME
WITH NO OBLIGATION TO BUY—EVER

**FIND OUT WHAT YOUR SURPRISE GIFT IS
SEE INSIDE**

YOURS FREE FOR KEEPS!

Use the edge of a coin to rub off the box at right and reveal your surprise gift ➡

DEAR READER:

We would like to send you 4 Harlequin Presents just like the one you're reading plus a surprise gift — all **ABSOLUTELY FREE.**

If you like them, we'll send you 8 more books each month to preview. Always before they're available in stores. Always for less than the regular retail price. Always with the right to cancel and owe nothing.

In addition, you'll receive **FREE**...
• our monthly newsletter HEART TO HEART
• our magazine ROMANCE DIGEST
• fabulous bonus books and surprise gifts
• special-edition Harlequin Bestsellers to preview for ten days without obligation

So return the attached Card and start your Harlequin honeymoon today.

Sincerely

Pamela Powers

Pamela Powers
for Harlequin

P.S. Remember, your 4 free novels and your surprise gift are yours to keep whether you buy any books or not.

4 EXCITING ROMANCE NOVELS PLUS A SURPRISE GIFT

FREE BOOKS/ SURPRISE GIFT

YES, please send me my four **FREE** Harlequin Presents® and my **FREE** surprise gift. Then send me eight brand-new Harlequin Presents each month as soon as they come off the presses. Bill me at the low price of $1.75 each (for a total of $14.00 – a saving of $1.60 off the retail price). There are no shipping, handling or other hidden costs. There is no minimum number of books I must purchase. I can always return a shipment and cancel at any time. Even if I never buy a book from Harlequin, the four free novels and the surprise gift are mine to keep forever.

108 CIP CAKA

NAME_____

ADDRESS_____APT. NO._____

CITY_____

STATE_____ZIP_____

Offer limited to one per household and not valid for present subscribers. Prices subject to change.

Mail to:

Harlequin Reader Service
901 Fuhrmann Blvd.
P.O. Box 1394
Buffalo, NY 14240
U.S.A.

LIMITED TIME ONLY
Mail today and get a SECOND MYSTERY GIFT

'But ...' she whispered and found she couldn't go on.

His eyes travelled over her meditatively. 'Why did I go out of my way to deny it?' he murmured. 'Is that what you were going to say? Because,' he went on without giving her a chance to speak although that wasn't what she'd been about to say, 'of anger and revulsion. I thought I had you taped as one of those merciless bitches who take advantage of something they've never earned. And because I also prefer to make an intellectual decision about those kind of things. I've found it's ... safer.'

Lineesa felt her heart move in her breast and she thought with a curious pang, that it felt as if it was dying. I've been tried and found wanting, she thought shakenly and confusedly, on the very level I was talking about—as a person, not just as a body and a face. How ironic? But why do I feel as if it's the final irony?

She licked her lips and made an effort to think of something to say. But the only thing that came to mind was a wish that the baby beneath her hand would wake up so that she could lift it into her arms and hold it ...

Then he said, 'Lin, can *I* tell you about Piers?'

'You don't have to.' Her voice was very low and she couldn't bring herself to look at him.

'Yes I do. I owe you that much at least. To try and make you understand why I was so ... the way I was. Piers was a lot younger than I was. And not long after he was born, our mother died.'

'But ...' Lineesa looked up involuntarily. 'I thought—I mean, Piers spoke of his mother ...'

'His stepmother,' David said expressionlessly. 'My father remarried when Piers was very young. She was neither a good wife nor a good mother although my father never saw that until it was too late. But Piers was the one who suffered for it mostly. Bronwen and I were older, you see. And that's why I felt more than normally protective of him, I guess.'

Lineesa said, 'I see . . .'

'But there's something else I have to tell you, something I should have told you a long time ago, Lin. Piers was . . . infatuated with speed. He always drove as if he was at Le Mans.'

'I know,' she breathed. 'But he was a good driver all the same.'

'All the same,' David repeated, 'there was a patch of oil on the road the night he died. And he wasn't a good driver, Lin. Oh, he could handle a car brilliantly, but he took the kind of chances good drivers don't take. He never allowed for the unpredictable.'

'What are you *saying*?' Lineesa asked at last.

'I'm saying . . . it was always on the cards that Piers would kill himself one day. He didn't need any provocation to be reckless on the road. Do you know why he bought that car? The car in the advertisement? Apart from trying to impress you with that particular model, he bought it because he'd written off his last car—the third one he'd written off in five years.'

Lineesa stared at him and started to shake. 'Why—why didn't you tell me?' she whispered.

David returned her gaze thoughtfully. 'I wanted to make you suffer, all the same, Lin,' he said finally. 'He was more serious about you than anything I've ever seen him be about anything. He grew up with a certain understandable cynicism about women. But in you, it was as if he'd found a cure for it. And even if he hadn't died, I'd have wanted to make you suffer for ... giving him that and then taking it away from him.'

Lineesa closed her eyes and leant her head back against the wall. She was no longer crying, it was as if her grief and hurt was too great for tears even. She didn't move when he spoke again.

'I'm sorry, Lin. It was ... unforgivable to accuse you of causing his death,' he said evenly.

'That's all right,' she murmured.

'It can't ... look at me, Lin.' His voice was suddenly harsh.

She opened her eyes and turned her head unwillingly. 'It can't be all right,' he said less harshly. 'Especially in the light of what you've told me.'

'Why?' She found it hard to speak. 'I haven't really told you anything you didn't know. I've only confirmed what you did know. I ... *let* Piers think ...'

'But not quite in the way I presumed it was,' he interrupted tautly.

She sighed. 'Perhaps not,' she said wearily. 'David, I'm tired. Can we ... just leave it be?' Her lips trembled, but she added resolutely. 'Please don't think I don't appreciate what you've told me, I do. But nothing on earth can change ... some things now, and I think it's best if we—leave them be. After all it's a small miracle that you and I should have come this far.'

'If you promise me one thing,' he said abruptly after a long time during which he'd stared at her white, strained face, then looked away with a frown in his blue eyes.

'What?'

'Forget about Piers now. It happened—the way it happened was nobody's fault but his own.'

The rain had stopped, she realised, in the silence

that followed his words, and a low, moaning wind had sprung up to take its place.

'Lin?'

She looked across at him and smiled, a haunting smile full of sadness that made him catch his breath, unbeknown to her. 'I'll try,' she murmured. 'I don't know how to make oneself forget though. But I'll try . . .'

And she turned away from him and slid down on to the mattress and pulled one of the thin blankets around her.

But she didn't sleep for a time. Instead she stared at the opposite wall with a faraway look in her eyes and a strange sense of knowledge in her heart. That dark, hidden depth of my soul, she thought suddenly, is not so hidden now. I've tried to deny to myself ever since it first happened, that David Marchmont means anything to me, to deny that he affects me in a way that I thought it was no longer possible to be affected by any man. But I should have known that he couldn't have hurt me or made me suffer so much, otherwise. If you don't care how you stand in someone's esteem, they can't hurt you that way, can they? But even now, when he's absolved me of Piers' death, I feel as if I'm just as much at his mercy as I ever was. And the knowledge that he . . . summed me up too, and discarded me on an intellectual level, and never revised that, is as much of a burden as Piers . . . oh God! Why did it have to be him . . . of all the men I turned away from, why does he have to be the one, I can't? At least not in my heart . . .

She fell asleep without knowing it.

CHAPTER FIVE

MORNING brought a new world.

Lineesa stretched and yawned as the baby began to move restlessly, and she blinked at the bright, early morning light coming through the windows.

She looked around but there was no sign of David and his mattress was already stowed in the small bedroom, she saw through the open door.

She got up and put two pans of water on to the stove to boil and opened the fire door to add wood, but realised David must have already done it. She wondered where he was.

And while she waited for the water to boil, she went to the front door and opened it—and stared out entranced at what she saw. Raindrops glittered like diamonds in the early sunlight, in the long grass and in the feathery foliage of the black-trunked acacia trees, and the air was so clear, from her raised vantage point, she could see for miles and the flat landscape was delicately tinted with the colours of the rising sun so that it looked like a Japanese print. And even the ugly surrounds of the homestead were less ugly, made so by the quality of light.

And as she watched, two kangaroos hopped through the rain spangled grass, only about a hundred yards from the house and stopped with their ears twitching as a flight of enormous birds with huge wings crossed the sky in front of the sun and shattered the stillness with their loud cries. Then the kangaroos took off too, in great leaps and disappeared.

I wonder if those birds were brolgas, Lineesa thought, and turned indoors as the baby began to make little cries, lest its small hungry presence be overlooked.

'Coming, Rosebud,' Lineesa murmured.

She made up the bottle and while it was cooling, washed herself as best she could in some of the rain water she'd warmed and changed into a clean pair of jeans and a lilac coloured cotton blouse. She brushed her hair and tied it back.

'Now it's your turn, pet,' she said to the baby and laid it on a towel on the table. 'This is what they call topping and tailing, I'm told. Not as much fun as a bath I'm sure but enough to make you clean and sweet for your bottle! I know, I know!' she said as the baby began to protest heartily. 'But I'll be as quick as I can!'

'There,' she said a few minutes later, 'washed and brushed and changed. Doesn't that feel better.' She reached for the bottle and tested the milk on the inside of her wrist. 'All right! All right!' She sat down and settled the now desperate baby in her arm and touched the teat of the bottle to its mouth. And the woeful expression on the little face changed immediately and she stopped crying mid-sob and began to suck contentedly.

'And to think of all the fuss you made yesterday, sweetheart,' Lineesa said in gentle mock-reproach. 'As if this bottle was the very last thing. . . .' She stopped abruptly and felt her skin prickle and looked up to see David standing in the doorway.

A faint colour tinged her cheeks and her heart moved in the curious way only he seemed to be able to make it, and she tensed inwardly at these involuntary reactions and forced herself to say calmly, 'Hello. I wondered where you were.'

He shrugged. 'Out and about. I thought you might be able to sleep in.' His eyes travelled over her, taking in the fresh blouse and jeans and coming back to rest on her face.

'I ... seem to have acquired a self-winding alarm clock,' she answered with a faint grin. 'I don't think babies ever sleep in.'

'They also ... suit you,' he said sombrely. 'When you're talking to that baby, you look happier, more at ease than I've seen you look for a long time.'

She said after a moment, 'Well, that's one good thing about babies I suppose. They can't talk back to you. They ... I mean. ...' She stopped and looked fleetingly confused.

'Would you like one of your own?' he said abruptly.

The question took her quite unawares. 'I ... one day, yes,' she stammered. 'But ...'

He waited.

'Well you can't have them in a vacuum, can you?' she managed to say wryly.

He looked at her searchingly. Then he said, 'No, but I can recommend you for motherhood.'

'Thank-you,' she murmured and looked down. Who to? she wondered. That's going to be the problem ...

Later, over breakfast of tinned baked beans and biscuits, he said. 'I should imagine there'll be a chopper arriving shortly. We'll go back to Windorah with it.'

'Oh?'

'Yes. After that rain we'll only get bogged if we try to drive on. In fact I think we'll be wasting our time going to Karendale now. It'll take days for the channels to subside so we won't be able to drive around.'

'Then, will we go home?' she asked with a swift upward glance.

'Is that what you want to do?'

She moved her hands restlessly. It was the last thing she wanted to do, she realised. 'It's up to you,' she said quietly.

He didn't answer her.

And half an hour later his prediction was proved correct. A State Emergency Services helicopter arrived with a doctor on board and the news that the Mullers were on the road to recovery in the Toowoomba Base Hospital, that it had been food poisoning they were suffering from and that they were frantic about their baby. But a message was immediately sent on the helicopter's radio to allay their fears and the doctor said to Lineesa. 'Not only well but blooming by the look of things, is Baby Muller. You must be a very resourceful lady, Mrs Marchmont!'

'Oh no,' Lineesa replied but couldn't help feeling warm inside. 'Anyone would have been able to cope.'

But when they landed at Windorah and she had to surrender the infant to the doctor who was accompanying it in the helicopter to Toowoomba, she didn't feel quite so warm inside. In fact as she hugged the baby for the last time and murmured, 'Goodbye, Rosebud,' her throat was clogged with tears and she turned away hurriedly after she'd handed the little bundle over only to find David standing right behind her with a sudden look of compassion and understanding in his eyes. And he put his arm around her shoulders and drew her close to him.

'Don't cry,' he said.

But she did shed some tears into his shoulder before managing to take a grip on herself. Then she looked up and sniffed and said huskily, 'I'm happy too. Sad and happy—things could have turned out much worse . . .'

But her words got caught in her throat at something in his eyes. Something that made her nerves tighten because she'd never seen it before, never thought to see it for her, a look that was nakedly intimate, the kind of look that a man directed to a woman he found desirable. And she trembled at the intensity of it as well as the unexpectedness of it . . . if he'd felt like that once about her as he'd said he had, she'd assumed those feelings had long since gone.

But what she saw next, hurt her as if he'd plunged a knife into her heart. She saw his lips tighten and his eyes narrow with something like disgust—as if he was disgusted at himself. And she knew that he was and she knew why . . . because he'd fleetingly fallen prey to a purely physical spasm of the senses, a thing he preferred not to do, he'd said. And least of all with me, she thought.

Then he released her and the world seemed to spin round once in a mad revolution, and she wondered briefly if she'd finally come apart . . . if it hadn't all, at last, become too much for her as it seemed to have been threatening to do lately.

But everything steadied and she heard him saying dryly, 'Yes, things could have been much worse . . .'

And she knew that he wasn't talking about the Muller's predicament.

That's why it came as such a surprise to her when they took off from Windorah an hour later, and headed north-east, instead of south for Sydney and Marchmont.

He'd said nothing about his plans during the hour they'd been on the ground. He'd spoken to

Karendale on the radio and arranged for a message to be relayed to Sydney.

'My mother?' she'd said.

'She doesn't know what happened. It didn't hit the press but in case it does now I've asked for Mike Smith to go and see her.'

'Oh . . .'

And when they were in the air and she realised the direction they were taking, she said tentatively, 'Aren't we going home?'

'Not just yet,' he said with the same cool sort of indifference that had marked his manner since that curious embrace on the airfield.

'Where then?'

'I thought of Shute Harbour. On the Whitsunday Passage. Have you ever been there?'

'. . . No.'

'It's very beautiful.'

She pressed her hands together. 'David . . . why are you doing this?' she asked with some difficulty.

'Because I promised you a holiday, and so far, haven't exactly provided one,' he said without looking at her.

She watched his hands as he checked the instrument panel, and knew she couldn't dent his containment and that it was hopeless to even try. It was as if they were back to the old days, as if they'd never spent the last three days in amiable companionship, for the most part.

Then why, she wondered with an inward shiver, *is* he doing this?

She still hadn't found an answer to that question when they were installed in a luxury motel overlooking Shute Harbour and the unbelievable beauty of the Whitsunday Passage that lies off the coast of Central Queensland adjacent to the sugar town of Proserpine.

'It's ... fantastic,' she murmured as she stood on the wide, private veranda of their suite and watched the setting sun to the west turn the peaceful waters of the Passage to a living orange. 'What island is that?' she asked.

'Daydream,' David said. 'It's the closest and the smallest of the resort islands. Whitsunday is the largest, Haymen probably the most famous but it's further out. Then there's Lindeman Island, South Molle ... we'll hire a boat tomorrow or the next day and do a tour. The coral around some of the islands is unbelievable. You can walk through it, with shoes on, and it's like walking through a garden and there's an under-water observatory off Hook Island. The fish are as often as exotic as the coral. Would you like to go out for dinner tonight, or have it up here?'

She turned. 'I don't think I've got anything to wear, other than jeans. Mrs Livingstone said that was all I'd need. I don't even think I've got a bathing-suit.'

'We can remedy that tomorrow. But there's a fish restaurant right on the wharf which wouldn't, I'm sure, take exception to jeans. Especially not with you in them,' he added with a mocking little smile.

She turned away defensively, and thought, so it is going to be like that ... Back to the old ways. But why? If I'm not to be punished for Piers anymore, why?

She bit her lip and fumbled with one of her bags, determined not to show her distress but with that painful query etched in her mind. And the answer to it that came from nowhere, almost took her breath away. She saw in her mind's eye with a fleeting but desperate clarity, what she'd seen in his eyes on the airfield, that brief flaring of desire that had been so totally unexpected. Is that it, David? she wondered. Am I to be punished now because you held me in your arms and found you still wanted me yourself, in spite of everything. And you hated that . . .? Oh no . . .

She straightened and found she'd broken out in a cold sweat.

'Lin?'

She bit her lip, then forced herself to turn around and say calmly, 'All right. But I'll change into a clean pair. Which . . .' She looked around. The suite consisted of a bedroom, bathroom and large livingroom that opened on to the paved terrace.

'You take the bedroom,' he said. 'This divan is made up as a bed beneath the fancy drapery. I'll use that. But there's no hurry . . .'

But over the next two days, it wasn't as she feared it would be, at least not quite. Yet neither were they as they'd been for the first three days of the so-called holiday. If anything they were more like two polite strangers who'd found themselves thrown together unexpectedly and were determined to make the best of it.

And he set such a cracking pace—they did hire a boat, and they did see all the islands and the coral, and they swam and fished and went sight-seeing on the mainland too, to Airlie Beach just up the road from Shute Harbour where David insisted she buy several dresses to augment the other item of clothing she'd purchased at Shute Harbour, an aquamarine one piece bathing suit—that she was too tired at night to do more than fall asleep, deeply and dreamlessly.

And they were so rarely in their motel suite at other times, she was spared any embarrassment there.

But there was an insidious strain to those three days, nevertheless. For all the activity they indulged in and all the polite conversation they made—she thanked God once, that there was so much to talk about and enthuse and marvel about—they were also closer in a purely physical sense than at any time since their wedding. Sitting next to each other in the car he'd hired, together on the speed boat he'd hired, swimming together in the sea or the motel pool, walking through the coral gardens together . . . it was impossible for her not to be aware of his body and the way he moved; and after twelve months of clamping down on every emotion but hatred for David Marchmont, she found she could do it no longer. It was as if, since admitting the terrible truth to herself on that rain-soaked night beyond Cooper Creek, that some inner floodgates of longing had been opened that she could no longer control. And the sight of his lean tall body that moved with such precision and did everything so well, stirred reactions in her own body that she only hoped and prayed he never guessed at.

Then she realised, sometime in the course of those three days, that he was being as scrupulous as she was in the matter of them not touching each other, even accidentally. And she couldn't help wondering with a sense of fear, if it was for the same reason that she was afraid to touch him— because she was afraid of betraying herself, afraid that he would feel how she sometimes trembled and felt hot and cold with a primitive yearning to feel his hands on her, and his lips . . .

If it is that, if he is still . . . physically attracted to me, he must hate me even more, to be in conflict with himself like this. I saw that look of disgust in his eyes, I didn't imagine it . . .

*   *   *

On the third night of their stay at Shute Harbour, they dined at Airlie Beach and drove back—silently for once—through the moonlight to the motel.

It wasn't very late, and Lineesa found she wasn't sleepy and wondered if she was getting used to this intense exposure to sea, sunlight and fresh air.

She wandered out on to the terrace to drink in the beauty of the moon on the water, and found it strangely intoxicating. Or perhaps it was the wine she'd drunk at dinner, three glasses of it which exceeded her normal quota by two ... and she wondered curiously why she'd had those extra glasses. Because of a growing sense of desperation? she asked herself and shrugged. Not that it's made me feel any different just—a little reckless? No, not even that, she mused. Relaxed?

She turned her head as she heard a footstep behind her and saw the moonlight shine on David's fair hair.

Well, she reflected with a certain wryness, this will be the test, won't it? If I don't launch into a variation of the seemingly millions of meaningless words I've uttered over the past three days, and if I don't find some excuse to go inside even although I don't want to go in ... then I'll know I'm feeling relaxed. Or is it reckless after all? Oh hell, she thought wearily, and with an abrupt movement, sat down on the stone coping of the terrace wall and stared out over the water with its iridescent sheen of moonlight that was like a net of silver.

She heard a match scrape and turned her head to see that David was leaning back against the dividing wall and that he'd lit one of the cigars he occasionally smoked after dinner. He still wore the cream jacket over the navy-blue sports shirt and trousers he'd worn to dinner, and although she couldn't see his features clearly, it was as if she knew them off by heart. The tanned lines of his face and throat, the way he narrowed his blue eyes when he drew on a cigar, his long, strong hands as he held it . . .

And suddenly she felt as if she was suffocating, as if her heart was beating too fast and all her pulses clamouring . . .

And she jumped up to go indoors with clumsy, uncoordinated movements that were quite alien to her.

But his voice stopped her.

'Don't go, Lin,' he said quietly and without turning his head.

'I . . . I have to,' she answered unsteadily, and clenched her fists so that her nails dug into her palms.

He turned his head then. 'Why?'

'I . . . I . . .' she faltered, and then her shoulders slumped slightly and her hands unclenched and she said barely audibly, 'You know why, David.'

The tip of his cigar glowed and the drift of the aromatic smoke from it wafted ethereally against the midnight blue backdrop of the night sky, before he spoke. 'Yes. You're running away from . . . me, Lin.'

She closed her eyes and her head dropped so that her hair which she'd left loose, fell over her face and she stood like that for a few moments. Then she raised her head and stared at him and it was as if there was an electric, magnetic field of tension between them as their eyes locked.

'Not . . . precisely,' she said in a low, husky voice. 'I'm running away from the fact that if . . . you're attracted to me . . .' She broke off as he moved abruptly but only to tip some ash off his cigar.

She licked her lips as he looked at her enquiringly. '. . . If you are . . .' She swallowed.

He smiled, a dangerously cool movement of his lips. 'There's no if about it, my dear,' he said idly. 'As I think you must be well aware. Go on.'

'Then,' she whispered, 'I'm running from the fact that you hate yourself for feeling like this about me, and that it doesn't really change what you feel for me—intellectually. That's never changed, has it, David?'

His eyes narrowed. 'Why are you so sure of that?' he said intently.

'I'm not blind,' she answered drily. 'I may be a lot of things but—not that.'

'All right,' he said after a moment, and she winced inwardly, 'assuming you're right about that, what about you?'

'What about me?'

'Well, you've catalogued *me* very neatly,' he said pleasantly. 'I thought you might like to describe *your* state of mind—and body. Or is it up to me to return the compliment?'

'David . . .'

'I'll do the best I can,' he drawled and tossed his cigar over the wall, 'although not as ably as you've turned me inside out, I'm afraid. Because I have to confess I often don't know what's going on inside that beautiful head of yours, Lin, and wouldn't like to guess . . .'

She moved sharply, to cut off his words and stumbled towards the doors that led into the living room, but he straightened and was beside her in two strides and he caught her wrist and swung her round to face. '*Don't* do that,' he said through his teeth. 'It's neither adult nor well-mannered.'

She took a breath and a nerve beat visibly in her
jaw line and a spark of anger lit her hazel eyes. 'I
don't have to stay to be insulted,' she said with an
effort. 'I don't find *that* particularly adult or well-
mannered. I'm sorry if you find that you still hate
and despise me but it wasn't my idea to force this
. . .' she lifted her free hand expressively to take in
the motel, the place, and the last three days, 'this
kind of battle of nerves on us. I thought,' her voice
cracked, 'I thought we'd achieved some sort of . . .
peace. We should have left it at that,' she said
bitterly.

'Like a pair of ostriches?' he said ironically.

'*Yes!*' she blazed and tried to twist her wrist free,
to no avail.

'No, Lin,' he said very softly but with a look of
menace in his eyes. 'That's not going to be good
enough for me. I told you I'd only call it quits
when I got to the bottom of you. But if you can
tell me, and convince me, that you didn't try to
scuttle inside a little while ago because it's a
torment to you too . . . *this*,' he said and released
her wrist and pulled her into his arms, 'I'll call it
quits now.'

'David . . . no,' she said shakily and brought her
hands up to push him away but he only smiled
slightly and slid one hand through her hair and
tugged gently so that she was forced to lift her
face.

'Lin, yes,' he murmured. 'Do you wonder what
it would be like to kiss me? Do you lie awake at
night and wonder what it would be like if we made
love? I have lately I must confess. I've wondered
all sorts of things about you . . . Whether you like
it to be gentle and slow, or whether you prefer a
savage lover. Whether you're generous and like to
give pleasure, or just to receive it. When you're so

beautiful I suppose it's natural to feel you're bestowing something special just by allowing yourself to be taken by a man ... You see, I've thought of all those things. And I think the time's come to ... find out ...'

'No,' she said on a breath and tried to turn her head away but his lips found hers unerringly. And she kept her mouth clamped shut, but he only laughed in his throat after a moment and began to kiss her eyelids, her cheeks and the hand that was in her hair, moved to the nape of her neck to press through the heavy strands of her hair, and then to slide round to the base of her throat, to lie there, stroking her slender neck just gently until she shivered suddenly down the whole length of her body, and she said again. 'No ... please!'

'Kiss me, Lin.'

'I don't ...'

'You have the most perfect skin. It's like caressing a piece of satin. Open your mouth, Lin ...'

'I don't like kissing ...'

'You should. Your mouth, your lips are made for it. They look so cool, so delicately curved, it's an invitation to plunder and pillage,' he said against the corner of her mouth.

She shivered, remembering the plunder and pillage he'd spoken of and how she'd hated it. But he didn't press her when she kept her lips shut. Instead, he slid the hand from around her throat, across her shoulder and down her back so that both his arms were around her hips, and he moulded the lower half of her body to him so that when she tried to pull away, all she succeeded in doing was leaning backwards against his arms, which he took advantage of to kiss the exposed line of her throat and the hollows at the base of her neck and the smooth rounded curves of her shoulders that the simple blue dress with shoestring straps, which she'd purchased at Airlie Beach, exposed.

'David ...' she whispered shakenly as his wandering lips caressed her skin.

'Mmm ...?' He raised his head briefly to send her a pure blue look from beneath half-closed lids.

'I ...'

'Don't like this either?' he said with an ironic little smile. 'Tell me another, Lin.'

And as she made a small sound of exasperation he covered her lips with his own and moved his hands on her, and her mouth trembled beneath his and her lips parted ...

But if it was plunder and pillage she expected, it wasn't what she got. It was something strangely beautiful and delicate, an act of intimacy that made her stunningly aware that she could participate—that she wanted to, in fact she did.

And when it ended finally, and he lifted his head, she stared up at him bemusedly, lingeringly, her eyes flickering to his mouth then back to his eyes.

'Was that so bad?' he said softly.

'No.'

'Then shall we ... go on from there?'

She swallowed. Why not? she thought.

'After all, it can't be such a momentous thing—for either of us, can it?' he said very quietly.

Can't it? she thought. 'I ... don't know,' she whispered.

'Then there's only one way to find out ...'

'I ... guess so ...'

'Lin,' he said later, 'what's wrong?'

She shivered. They were lying on the double bed in the bedroom and the moonlight coming through

the window was turning his fair hair to silver. It
had been all right, she thought hazily, when he'd
undressed her. It had been a thing of quivering,
leaping senses, a mindless sort of delight only
faintly tinged with apprehension. It had been
compulsive too. His wandering, caressing hands
had seen to that. And something in his eyes when
he'd looked down at her, free of her clothes, had
added to it. It was as if he was saluting her. But
he'd said then, 'You're so very lovely . . .' And his
voice hadn't been quite steady.

And she'd thought then, lovely . . . love . . .
sex—that's what this is. Not love . . .

And she'd stiffened and the delight had become
more and more like apprehension and a correspond-
ing withdrawal . . .

'Lin?' His voice brought her back.

'I'm sorry,' she whispered. 'I don't want to do
this. I'm not very good at . . . it,' she stammered.

He raised his head. And in the moonlight his
eyes were more shockingly cynical than she'd ever
seen them. 'You . . . bitch,' he said with a world of
contempt. 'But it's too late, Lin. Too late to
change your mind now . . .'

The moonlight had gone.

And in its place was the light of the bedside
lamp, a queer, blue sort of light that made the
white walls of the motel bedroom seem whiter.

Blue lampshades, she thought, don't shed a very
comforting light . . .

She moved uncertainly and was surprised to find
she was covered by a sheet. I don't remember that.
What do I remember? No dizzy heights, no bells,
no . . . ecstasy. I always suspected it was
exaggerated, what I read about sex . . . so many
words to describe it. Lovely . . . no not that. Just a

bruised, aching feeling. A used sort of feeling. And so tired . . .

'Lin?'

She turned her head. David was sitting beside the bed with his trousers on and his shirt, but it looked as if it had been pulled on carelessly and was unbuttoned and the collar awry. She closed her eyes.

'Why didn't you tell me?' he asked on a curiously uneven note.

She licked her strangely dry lips and opened her eyes to find herself staring up at the ceiling—a different ceiling, without the moulded cornice and stippled effect of her bedroom at Marchmont. 'You—would you have believed me?' she whispered.

He said roughly, 'Raping virgins is not one of my proudest accomplishments . . . You could have tried me.'

I could have, she thought hazily. I don't know why I didn't. Maybe it was because you assumed I wasn't a virgin, you *always* took that for granted, David. So what does that mean? A Freudian attempt to get my own back . . .?'

'I'm sorry,' she said desolately.

There was silence for a bit. Then he said very quietly, 'No, I'm sorry.' And he reached over to smooth a strand of her hair and tuck it behind her ear, and she looked down from the ceiling, directly into his eyes.

It was a long, sober look and it contained something more direct than anything that had ever flowed between them, a new knowledge—a bond that had been forged even if by misdeed and in misapprehension. And she trembled visibly and tried to speak but with no clear idea of what she was going to say.

He waited. Then when it became obvious that
the words weren't going to come, he smiled
twistedly and said, 'You look so very young. I
often forget how young you are, you're usually so
poised. If ... you could talk about it, if you could
talk to me and *tell* me how it's been for you, it
might help us both.'

She pleated the sheet between her fingers for a
long time, and her eyes were shadowed and
confused. Then she said hesitantly, 'I ... suppose I
was a bit more naïve than most. I *thought* I was
everything that was modern and progressive—you
know how it is when you're seventeen, you think
you know everything ... But I soon found out
that I didn't. And I discovered that I'd ...
subconsciously, imbibed more of my mother's old-
fashioned notions than I'd ever realised. So that
when men,' she swallowed, 'started to take an
interest in me, at first I was flattered and I suppose
... flirtatious.' She grimaced. 'But it wasn't very
long before that changed and if anything I became
... I sort of felt a revulsion. I found I didn't enjoy
being kissed and mauled for the price of a dinner.
Nor did I like being in a constant state of wariness
in case I got trapped into a situation I couldn't get
out of ... you may not realise,' she said bitterly,
'how clever some men are at turning the most
innocent occasion, seemingly, into a scenario for
seduction.'

'Go on,' he said after a little while.

She sighed and moved her head restlessly. 'I
went through a few different stages of ...
disillusionment, I suppose you could say. I
thought at one time, that there was something
wrong with *me*. Maybe I was frigid. Then I
thought, at one stage, why not get it over and done
with? Why not go to bed with someone I didn't

particularly dislike. Everyone else seems to be doing it all the time ... But that led me into a situation I shall never forget, nor will I ever forget the guilt and embarrassment of it. Because I ended up climbing out of his ... this man's bedroom window and down a drainpipe, to my everlasting shame ...'

He looked fleetingly amused. But he said. 'Did the revulsion get the upper hand?' And his eyes were sombre and intent then.

'No ... Not really. He was rather nice and ... but I knew it wouldn't lead to anything more than a—pleasant little interlude for both of us and I suddenly felt ... tawdry and cheap. And I just couldn't do it. Then I found I felt cheaper, if anything, for deliberately letting him expect it and then at almost the last minute, running out on him ... and like that too. And that led to another stage in the process. I began to feel disillusioned with myself as much as anyone, and I began to understand that I was in a sense, responsible for what was happening to me. That I was inviting men to think of me only in those terms of taking me to bed, it was my trade ...'

'Did you never think of getting out of—your trade, as you put it?' he queried.

'Yes, often. But you see, I'd set myself a goal ...'

'Your mother's house?'

'Yes, and the other things she'd gone without for so long. And that goal was coming closer and closer in lots of respects, but further away in others. Once I'd saved the deposit on the house, I thought I'd achieved so much. Then I realised that to keep up the repayments well ...' She shrugged. 'There was nothing else I was trained to do.'

He was silent and she watched him but couldn't

tell what he was thinking. And she said huskily, at last, 'I often thought it was a ... curious paradox. To appear to be the embodiment of the thing I was least good at, least able to handle or understand.'

'Lin,' he said abruptly, and stopped.

'What were you going to say?' she whispered after a moment.

His eyes flickered over her face narrowly but he didn't answer.

'Were you ...' she swallowed, 'going to ask me how it all fits in with tonight? Going to ask me why I didn't climb out of a window and down a drainpipe tonight?'

He closed his eyes briefly. 'I didn't give you much chance to do anything like that ...'

'Because you didn't know,' she whispered.

'You don't have to make excuses for me, Lin,' he said with a sudden savagery and his eyes dark.

'I think I do. You see, when you asked me why I didn't at least *try* to tell you, I realised that one of the reasons was that deep down, I was angry because you'd never once stopped to think that I might be a virgin. And in a foolish, childish way I guess,' tears glittered in her eyes, 'I thought, well I'll *show* him ...'

They stared at each other until he said in a low voice, 'And the others ... you said, *one* of the reasons ...?'

She gripped the sheet tightly. 'I—in a way, I felt as if I was paying my debt for Piers. For all the things I've done wrong that led up to ... Piers.' Her voice shook and was tinged with a sort of wonder. 'Yes,' she added barely audibly and made no attempt to stem the flow of silent tears that streamed down her cheeks.

'Hell ...' he said on a breath and stood up, only to sit down on the side of the bed and gather her up into his arms. 'Don't, Lin,' he murmured over the top of her head as she wept into his shoulder. 'I feel bad enough as it is. I'm *sorry*,' he held her away from him and searched her wet face with frowning, sombre eyes, 'I'm sorry,' he said more gently, 'for everything, but especially for making you feel you had to pay your debts that way. For even . . . for *ever* saying what I did about making you suffer. Because I didn't mean it to be this way. And I know now that I was wrong, that I've been wrong about you all the way through.' He rocked her in her arms as if she was a child until she quietened at last.

And lifted her tear-streaked face to his. 'Then,' she whispered, 'is this . . . finally the end? Can we c-call it quits now?' she said shakily.

He didn't speak for an age and she saw his lips tighten fleetingly and that his eyes were full of concern and a sort of torture. But what he said at last, took her breath away . . .

'Yes, we can call a halt to all the hostilities, finally. And start our marriage—finally.'

Her lips parted and her eyes widened incredulously. 'David . . .'

'You didn't think I'd let you go like this, did you, Lin?' His voice was suddenly harsh. 'I too, like to pay my debts . . .'

'But . . .' She found she couldn't go on, could only stare at him, stunned. Then she moved convulsively to free herself but he wouldn't let her.

'No, David,' she said then, pantingly. 'We can't . . . don't you see that we can't?' she added despairingly.

'Nevertheless, we will, Lin. Trust me a little.' He grimaced wryly. 'Perhaps that was the last thing I should say. But if you can, it will be all right . . .'

CHAPTER SIX

THE sunlight woke Lineesa the next morning as it had done on a day not so long ago, the day of her first wedding anniversary. And it was with a similar sensation that she blinked and sat up and looked around her. A sense of being totally over-burdened but not sure why. Then she remembered all that had happened the previous night and she lay back, for a moment wondering if she hadn't imagined it all.

But physically she was reminded that she hadn't imagined the first part of it at least, and she bit her lip and turned her head into the pillow.

Then she realised that she hadn't imagined any of it, because she remembered the futile protests she'd tried to make in answer to David's statement about their marriage—protests that had been as effective as knocking her head against a brick wall until she'd started to cry again and he'd brought her a glass of water, and lifted her back into his arms and soothed her until she'd fallen asleep.

'What am I going to do?'

The words escaped her involuntarily, as everything that had happened fell into place, and she had no idea that the shower had been running when she'd first woken, or that it had stopped while she'd been thinking, and that David had walked out of the bathroom in time to hear her say them.

In fact she only turned jerkily when she felt a presence instinctively, to see him standing beside the bed in a pair of shorts and with a towel in his hand that he was rubbing his wet hair with.

'What's wrong?' he said huskily. 'Are you in pain?'

'No. I mean—I'm all right.' She blushed and looked away.

'Not quite all right, I shouldn't imagine,' he said and sat down beside her. 'Don't look like that,' he added gently and touched her hot cheek, then turned her face towards him with his fingers beneath her chin. 'I only want to help. What you might be feeling now,' he said not quite evenly, 'should pass. But if it doesn't you must tell me. I might have done some damage . . .'

'No,' she interupted agitatedly. 'I'm all right! I didn't mean that.'

He studied her searchingly. 'Would you like a bath?' he said at last.

She stared up at him and nodded after a moment.

'I'll run you one.'

But he did more. He picked her up and carried her, sheet and all to the bathroom when the bath was ready, and stood her on the bathmat, still wrapped in it.

'David,' she said. But her voice got stuck in her throat.

'No, Lin,' he answered very quietly. 'If it's still what you were trying to say last night, I don't see how we can part like this. I *know* I can't. And if you just let yourself relax, you will see that we can . . . build something worthwhile out of this. Have your bath,' he added with a slight smile, and left her.

They stayed at Shute Harbour for another week. And for the first two days of that week, Lineesa felt as if she was in another world. They did more or less nothing by comparison to their rather frenzied activities of the preceding days. They swam in the motel pool and lazed beside it—and took up fishing. David purchased two rods and they fished off the jetty—at least David did so more constructively; Lineesa spent a lot of time watching the myriads of little fish that swam about beneath the planking, and watching the colourful throng of tourists that were Shute Harbour's livelihood as the main gateway to the Whitsunday Passage.

And he was as gentle with her as if she was a child, attentive and talkative, often funny—showing her the side of him she'd only known about indirectly for so long, and then experienced briefly somewhere between Cooper Creek and the Diamantina . . .

And it had the effect of gradually releasing her from the cocoon of shock and despair she'd been in, despite her inner conviction that this was as disastrous a course he'd set for them as any other he'd plotted. Where there wasn't love, only guilt, and that on both sides, how could they make a successful marriage?

She caught her breath as she found herself thinking that coherently for the first time, on the second day of the week. Only guilt, and that on *both* sides? Does that mean no love . . . *not* on both sides? Or put another way, love on one side but not the other? On my side . . .?

And she asked herself again how she could possibly think she loved David Marchmont. After everything that had happened did she still feel that old, haunting attraction, that curious desire to stand high in his estimation? And she thought, is that what love really is? Something quite unassailable that you're stuck with for the rest of your life in spite of everything? Surely not . . .

But only a few hours after thinking those thoughts, she found herself prey to another set that shook her and only seemed to confirm what she'd wondered.

There had been nothing particularly lover-like in David's attitude towards her since that night. What had passed between them that fateful night might not have occurred. He still slept in the lounge and accorded her the kind of privacy he always had until then, except for the time he'd undressed her at Marchmont. But he was not as scrupulous about not touching her as they'd both been before. If he thought she was cold when they'd been swimming, he wrapped her in a towel, and if he thought she needed a hand when they went fishing or walking, he held her hand quite naturally . . . it seemed to happen in a lot of different ways but it wasn't anything more than a father might do for a child . . .

At least that's what she'd felt until she reached that stage on the second day of being able to co-ordinate her thoughts, and she found herself watching him. They were fishing off the jetty. The sun was low in the western sky and the first of large tourist boats that took day trippers round the islands, was approaching with its load of happy, sun-burnt people who'd viewed the marvels of the coral, had a barbecue lunch on an island, maybe seen a whale in the passage.

David reeled his line in and said with a grin, 'We'll get caught in a traffic jam soon. Let's go . . . Here, I'll wind your line in. I don't think somehow, that I'm going to make a dedicated fisherwoman out of you, Mrs Marchmont. You're too much of a dreamer. I reckon you lost your bait half an hour ago.'

His eyes teased her and she found herself smiling back at him, and *watching* him with a sudden feeling of breathless confusion, as he stood up lithely. He was only wearing a pair of shorts and an old straw hat he'd had pressed on him by the motel owner so the grace and elegance of his tall sleek body was almost over-poweringly obvious. So was the easy strength and she remembered with a curious shiver how he'd used that unobtrusively yet undeniably powerful body to subdue her and . . .

You'd think, she reflected, that the last thing I'd want to do is have any reminder of that, let alone—want to reach over and touch him, and be thinking what I am thinking . . . that to have someone who you know could crush you and hurt you, treat you gently and with tenderness must be . . . special . . .

'Lin?'

Her eyes widened and she realised he was holding his hand down to her, to help her to her feet. She took it hastily but the contact sent an electric sensation up her arm and she trembled and knew that he must have felt it, because his blue eyes narrowed as he studied the wave of colour that came to her cheeks and the strange expression in her eyes, before she looked away uncertainly.

He didn't say anything, but the pressure on her hand increased briefly, then he let it go and they collected their gear in silence and walked back to the motel.

Dinner was strained that night when curiously, it hadn't been the night before, possibly because she'd been too numb to care. Yet tonight, she found herself wanting to make conversation but unable to think of anything to say.

She'd showered and changed since coming up from the jetty, into a pretty, long cotton dress in a grey and white small-floral print with a simple vee neckline and short, puffed sleeves. It was one of the dresses she'd bought at Airlie Beach, from a rack of identical ones in all but size but it was cool and comfortable and the green scarf that matched the flecks in her hazel eyes, with which she'd tied her hair back, contrasted well with the grey and white.

David had showered and changed too, into cream denim jeans and a brown silk sports shirt but with his fair hair now tamed and his whole groomed appearance, she found him a little frightening.

They'd had their meal sent up to them and it had come accompanied by flowers and candles. The owner-manager of the motel had not been unalive to the name of Marchmont and had taken every step possible to ensure that the bearers of that name had been as comfortable and well-looked after as possible—even to lending David his lucky fishing hat.

And the baked, freshly-caught Coral Trout had been superb, but the constraint had remained.

Lineesa had glanced at David several times in the candlelight, and opened her mouth to speak but had not done so because he hadn't been looking at her and his expression had been unfathomable.

And then, when they'd finished eating, she'd found herself feeling like Cinderella, tongue-tied, unreal and as if she was there by proxy . . .

And a shimmer of tears came to her eyes then and she looked down hastily and picked up her napkin simply for something to do, and knocked

over her wine glass which rolled off the table and
smashed on the quarry-tile floor.

She closed her eyes in exasperation and stood up
hurriedly but he said sharply, 'Don't.'

'I must,' she answered in muffled, mortified
tones, and bent down.

'Leave it, Lin. I'll get someone up to deal with it.'

His tones were so peremptory, she straightened
up uncertainly to see that his lips were set tautly
and his eyes hooded. 'Take your coffee on to the
terrace,' he added.

'A—all right,' she murmured helplessly and did
as she was bid.

He didn't come out to join her until a waiter
had been summoned to deal with the broken glass,
and also to remove the remains of the meal. Then,
when the door had finally closed behind him,
David strolled out on to the terrace and she was
able to glint him a fleeting, wry smile, and say,
'Sorry. That was clumsy of me.'

He set his own coffee cup down on the wrought
iron table and stared at her expressionlessly until
she turned away nervously.

Nor was her nervousness helped when she heard
him make an impatient sound, as if he was
swearing beneath his breath, and she tensed as she
heard him cross the tiles towards her, and she
wanted to run, to escape but knew he wouldn't let
her.

So it came as a complete surprise when he only
put his hands gently on her shoulders and said in
a strangely husky, uneven voice, 'I'm sorry, Lin,
so sorry...'

A tremor shook her and he felt it and his hands
tightened briefly. 'What for?' she whispered and
wished she had the courage to turn round and face
him. 'I thought you were . . . angry with me.'

'Not you,' he murmured and slid his hands down her arms and pulled her gently backwards into his arms, 'myself . . .'

She tried to turn then but his arms imprisoned her and he said in the same quiet voice, 'With myself for bringing back that look of strain to your eyes and your mouth, that haunted look. I thought—I was going to be able to erase it. I think now I must have been mad, and incredibly presumptuous to imagine that I, of all people, could ever do that. That you'll ever be able to look at me without remembering everything . . . I saw that in your eyes this afternoon.'

'Then . . . you're not a very good reader of eyes,' she said desolately and started to shake because she'd spoken without stopping to think, or to gauge the consequences, spoken from her heart.

He said after a moment and in a voice quite unlike his own and as if it was an effort to speak, 'Go on.'

'I c-can't,' she stammered. 'I shouldn't have said that. Please, let me go.'

'No,' he said roughly, 'not until you *tell* me what you meant, Lin.' He turned her round to face him.

'Is it,' he looked down at her intently and his eyes glittered strangely, 'can it be that I didn't kill the attraction you felt for me, stone dead? Is that what you don't want to tell me, Lin?'

She licked her lips and found that her heart was beating heavily and uncomfortably and her mind was in a terrible turmoil. If I admit that, she thought, I'll have nothing left to hide, nothing else to use as cover . . .

'Lin . . .' He said her name on a mere breath and touched her face with his fingers as if he was touching the petals of a flower.

Oh, don't do that, she cried, but inwardly. I don't

have any defences for gentleness and tenderness, don't you see?

'Lin, tell me,' he said very quietly. 'Don't hide it from me or try to run away from me again, *please*.'

She stared up at him and her lips quivered as he continued to stroke her face. Then she made a small, hoarse sound in her throat and said despairingly, 'Yes—I mean no, you didn't kill it stone dead, David. I knew that this afternoon. That's what you saw... but, you see, for both of us it can only be something physical so... and...'

'Shouldn't we reserve judgment on that, Lin?' he said after a long time during which their gazes had locked with a magnetic intensity.

'I ...' she whispered finally.

'I know. You don't like to confuse sex with love, very wisely.' He smiled slightly and traced the outline of her mouth with one finger. 'But I think it's got to be something more than a purely physical attraction we feel because we know each other rather well now. I mean, for me, it's not only a desire to possess a lovely body any more. It's ...' He stopped.

'What?' she said after a moment. 'Not love, I know that. But it could be a sense of guilt although it shouldn't be, David, because...'

'All the same it is,' he interrupted sombrely. 'But there's also a sense of admiration for the things I've come to know about you. For instance, when we were up in the channel country I sensed, and saw, a spirit of peace and serenity in you that few people achieve. And it was ... it reached out and touched me, like a calming raft and in an entirely unphysical way. Then there's your honesty, towards yourself. And there's the strange fact,' he paused and looked at her very directly, 'that even when I was being your jailer and accuser, I couldn't help feeling sometimes that you were a worthy prisoner and opponent. You were always so proud and defiant, I began to think I'd never break you—I didn't ever. I came close to breaking your health, but not your spirit. I don't know what to call it, admiration, respect, a desire to try and wipe out the wrong I did you, a desire to comfort you and love you and make you understand that where there's warmth and an expense of spirit between two people, it's not just simply sex . . . it's a communion too.'

She stared up at him and felt her throat close with unshed tears. So that it was only with great difficulty, that she managed to whisper, 'Thank-you for saying that.' And smile up at him with tears in her eyes.

A smile that made him close his eyes briefly as if it had hurt him, and pull her into his arms and bury his face into her hair.

They stood like that for an age. Then his hands moved on her and she shivered, not from fear but desire, and he picked her up and carried her inside.

'Did that hurt at all?' he said later, much later.

'No. It was . . . very nice.'

He touched her face. 'For me, it was sensational—as you might have gathered.' A smile lit his eyes. 'And one day it will be that way for you.'

She coloured faintly. 'I didn't mean . . . I . . .'

'I know what you meant,' he murmured and gathered her close. 'That special feeling that leaves you breathless and mindless isn't always automatic. It takes nurturing and I intend to nurture you until it comes. With your permission, naturally.' A spark of wickedness lit his blue eyes. 'May I count on that?'

'You may . . .'

He did just that.

He made her more conscious of her body and hitherto latent sensuality than she'd dreamt possible. And in more ways than she'd ever dreamt of . . .

'You're—I can't believe how beautiful you are,' he said, not quite steadily, once.

She looked up, surprised. They were having lunch at an open-air beer-garden and had spent the morning sailing in the Passage.

'But I'm a mess,' she said with a grimace. 'My hair is all tangled and full of salt and sand—so is the rest of me!' She glanced down ruefully at her shorts and T-shirt.

'I was hoping you'd say that,' he murmured in reply and added abruptly, 'Are you still very hungry?'

She blinked at him and looked down at her half-finished fisherman's basket. 'Why?'

'Because if you're not, I've thought of something else we could be doing. We could always eat later . . .'

'Well . . . if you want to.'

'I do. Come.' He stood up and held out his hand to her.

'Couldn't we do this "something else" later?' she queried with a sudden glint of suspicion in her eyes, as they arrived back at the motel rather precipitously.

'No, my dear Lin.' He closed the door behind them and she felt as if he was closing the rest of the world out rather than just closing the door. 'Unless you'd rather I died of starvation—of another kind. How does this thing come off?' he added as he reached for her and lifted the hem of her T-shirt.

'Over my head but . . .'

'That's terribly unromantic,' he grumbled. 'I'm sure T-shirts were invented for men not women. Lift up your arms!'

She did. 'David . . .' But her words got smothered as he pulled the offending T-shirt off. And when she emerged, it was to see him staring frustratedly at her one piece swimsuit which she had on beneath her shorts.

And she had to grin at his expression. 'All right, I understand,' she murmured. 'But you'll have to wait a while longer. I should take a shower, I'm all gritty with sand.'

He lifted his eyes to hers and said, 'I know.' And she took a startled breath at the naked look of desire she saw. He said, 'That's what I had in mind while I was watching you eat your lunch. I found myself thinking of you standing under the shower. Come,' he said again and took her hand.

'There,' he said a little later. 'I knew you wouldn't disappoint me . . .'

She stared up at him and found her breathing wasn't quite steady. Then she looked down at herself. They were both in the shower but while he was only wet, she was soapy too with the white foamy lather from the shampoo he was massaging into her hair, sliding down her golden body.

'Like that?' he murmured as his long, strong fingers probed her scalp gently.

'Yes . . .' She lifted her head and closed her eyes.

His hands slid down then, to her shoulders and her breasts, to linger fleetingly before continuing their gliding path to her waist and the slight soft curve of her stomach. And her body began to tingle in a way she couldn't describe.

'Can I . . .' She stopped and her eyes flew open.

'Can you what, Lin?' His voice was barely audible and his hands roamed over her hips and thighs.

'Can I do it to you?' she whispered.

'Sure . . .'

She did although she had to stand on tip-toe to reach his head and her breasts brushed against him and she felt him shudder suddenly and he pulled her into his arms and moved so that they were directly under the spray of water. And when the shampoo had been rinsed away, he kissed her deeply and their bodies entwined and the water flowed off them . . .

But what she was expecting, what her whole being seemed to be crying out for, didn't occur and she made a futile little sound when he lifted her off her feet suddenly and set her down outside the shower cubicle.

'Is something wrong?' she said huskily as he reached for a towel.

'No, very right,' he said and began to blot the moisture from her body and hair.

'I thought . . . I thought it was going to be love in the shower, this "something else" you wanted us to do,' she managed to say with a small teasing smile, to cover her disappointment.

'Oh that!' he said casually. 'No, I think it was just my unsuspected, long-sublimated desire to be a hair-dresser coming to the fore. We can go back to our lunch now, if you like.'

'David . . .'

But he was laughing. 'If you could see your face,' he said at last. 'No. That was just an appetizer, my lovely Lin. For what I have in mind now, we need a bed . . .'

'See what I mean,' he said very softly not much later.

She did although she hadn't expected to because it seemed as if the magical moment had passed. But when her cool body was resting on the smooth sheets of the bed, and he was lying beside touching her breasts until her nipples hardened and she drew up her legs sideways as a sudden tremor wracked her body, she found she was glad he'd waited . . .

'Yes. No . . . I . . .'

'No?' His voice was a little indistinct.

'I mean, yes, I see, and no, don't do that . . .'

'Don't you like me kissing your nipples?'

She looked down at the damp fair head so close to her breasts and closed her eyes. 'It's like,' she shivered as she felt his tongue slide across one taut peak, 'some kind of sweet torture,' she whispered.

'It is for me too. In the sense that I seem to spend nine tenths of my life nowadays wanting to inflict this sweet torture on you . . .'

'David,' she gasped a little later, 'please . . .'

And that had been the first time that she'd come close to the special feeling he'd described, and she'd been so sceptical of. Not that she cared that she hadn't quite reached it because his infinite pleasure in her had been enough to more than satisfy her.

But he said later. 'We're getting closer, I think.'

'How did you know?' she whispered with a faint tinge of colour in her cheeks.

He smiled slightly and pulled her back into his arms. 'I just do . . . Something in the way you move beneath me now. Are you . . . happy, Lin?' His eyes were serious as they probed hers.

Am I? she thought fleetingly. I'm not unhappy . . .

'Don't answer that,' he said after a moment as she hesitated.

'David,' she took a breath, 'yes I am.'

He studied her narrowly and she thought he was going to question what she'd said and felt herself tense slightly.

But in the end he only dropped a light kiss on her hair and said in a perfectly grave voice, 'You know, I've always felt mirrors on the ceiling are a waste of time.'

'Mir ... on the ceiling?' She looked at him a comical frown.

'Mmm. It took you to make me understand why people have them.'

'Me ... *do* people have them?'

'So I'm told. I've never actually seen one, or felt I've missed out on experiencing one. But I've just thought how much I'd enjoy lying here watching you ... us.' He grinned a little wickedly. 'You're shocked,' he commented.

'Yes,' she agreed. 'It sounds ... immoral somehow.'

'If you weren't so very beautiful, I might not get these immoral ideas,' he teased.

'Oh now! That's not fair ...' But he was laughing at her and she began to laugh too.

The next afternoon he went out to mail some letters including one she'd written to her mother, and arrived back with a new dress for her.

'But I don't need another dress,' she'd protested.

'You need this one.'

'Why?'

'There's a dance up at the pub tonight. I thought we'd go.'

'Well,' she looked at the plastic bag with the dress in it, wrapped in tissue paper, 'thank-you. I'll try it on.'

He grinned suddenly. 'No, don't do that.'

'What if it doesn't fit?'

'It will. I got it where you got the others. They remembered you. Most people do,' he added and something in his voice made her pause and look at him uncertainly.

He shrugged and said wryly, 'It's hard not to, Lin.'

'David . . .'

But he interrupted her. In fact he came over to her and took her into his arms, 'Yesterday, when you said, David, *please*, to me I'd have jumped off the Sydney Harbour bridge for you.'

'I think I was just about ready to do that myself,' she whispered. 'Why did you buy me a dress.'

But all he would say was, 'You'll see.'

She did see, but by degrees. The dress was the colour of vanilla ice-cream and the sleeveless bodice was ruched on either side into a placket that ran from the neck to below the waist and did up via the medium of twenty tiny pearl buttons. The colour looked stunning against her deepening tan and the skirt swirled around her legs from a lowered waistline.

'Like it?' he said when she was in it.

'Mmm.' She admired the dress in the mirror and wondered if she should have worn a bra. But the night was hot and muggy and the soft pleats of the bodice were quite concealing. She fingered a pearl button and looked at David to see him watching her carefully. 'Did you go looking for it? Or . . .'

'No. It was in the window. Put your hair up.'

'All right.' She reached for her brush.

'Don't you like it?' he said after a moment.

Lineesa looked down at herself in the pretty, fresh cotton dress and said indistinctly because of the hairpins in her mouth, 'I love it. It makes me feel . . . young . . .'

The dance was lively and whether because of her new dress that made her feel young and happy, or just because she was happy, she metaphorically let down her hair and joined in the spirit of things. They danced a lot and she laughingly refused other offers to dance to return time and time to David's arms. In fact as the night wore on it became harder to tear herself away from him even when the music wasn't playing.

It must be something to do with this dress, she thought once. And later, when the music was slow and dreamy and the lights very dim, she slid her arms round his neck with a queer little sound in her throat and tilted her head back as his hands came up to her shoulders. She closed her eyes and danced for a while in silence. Then her eyes flickered open to see that he was staring down at her and his gaze roamed from her lips to her breasts and she had a suddenly haunting vision of his long, strong fingers undoing each tiny pearly button and sliding his hands beneath her dress and freeing her breasts from the vanilla cotton . . .

A tremor shook her body and, for a blinding few moments, she forgot where she was and her eyes told him what she was thinking and that she'd lost all sense of time and place and wouldn't have been able or wanted to stop him from doing just as she'd imagined.

But a crash of cymbals brought her back and she felt a hot blush rising from the base of her throat. 'W-what are you doing to me?' she stammered.

He smiled slightly and gathered her close, 'Nothing that you don't do to me,' he murmured into her hair.

'Why did you buy this dress?' she whispered, although she already knew the answer.

'Because the minute I saw it, I thought how much I'd like to take it off you very slowly. That's why I wouldn't let you try it on . . .'

'Then,' she said huskily after a moment, 'you'd better take me home.'

'Oh?'

'Mmm . . . I've just thought of something else we could be doing.'

But although they left in the middle of that dance, when they were back at the motel, he took his time about taking the vanilla dress off her—as he always did when he made love to her, she thought dimly, took all the time in the world to kiss and caress her body until she was trembling from head to toe and aching with desire and ready and longing to accept his body into hers.

This time though, she felt a growing, urgent need to repay his consideration and patience. Felt it growing as he sat down on the settee and pulled her on to his lap and one by one undid the little buttons. Then when the paler, pearly skin of her breasts was still partly shadowed by the open front of her dress, he slid his fingers into her hair and pulled out the pins so that it tumbled down in a glorious cloud of sun-tipped gold. And only then did he push the dress wide open and touch her nipples.

She watched as they swelled and hardened like pink buds, and shivered at the flood of quivering sensation that surged through her body from her scalp to her toes.

Then she took an uncertain breath and linked her fingers round his wrists and stilled his hands. 'Wait,' she whispered.

His eyes lifted to hers.

'Please . . .'

He didn't say anything but his hands sank into her lap and she released his wrists after a moment and began to undo the buttons of his shirt. It took longer than it should have because her fingers weren't quite steady and seemed to fumble a lot. But finally it was open to his waist and she placed her hands palm downwards on his taut diaphragm and bent her head so that her hair swung over her breasts and kissed the smooth tanned skin at the base of his throat and slid her tongue round in small circles and tugged at it gently with her teeth and moved her hands lingeringly round his waist and up his back.

'Lin,' he said on a curiously uneven note but she lifted her head and placed her lips on his and timidly let her tongue slide across them.

He said something like, 'Oh God . . .' and began to kiss her deeply and not gently.

But when the kiss finished at last, it seemed she hadn't.

She lay in his arms breathing quickly for a few moments, then she slid off his lap and caught hold of his hand and tugged at it until he stood up and followed her into the bedroom. There she knelt down to undo his shoelaces and helped him to take off his clothes and he pushed her dress off and reached for her lacy briefs which were all she had left on.

Then she took his hand again and lay down on the bed and lifted it to her lips as he sat down beside her, and she kissed his palm and laid his hand across her breasts and slid her other hand up the length of his arm and down over his chest very slowly.

'I . . . you . . . make me want you so much,' she whispered. 'I want to do the same for you. Show me how . . .'

He did. And what followed was the most intense experience Lineesa had ever been part of. And at the climax of it, it was as if her body was transported into a spinning world of sensation that left her gasping and clinging to him as if he was the only anchor she had in this new world she was floating in, a world of space shot through with shuddering, infinite pleasure—a world that exceeded by far what she'd come to believe of it so sceptically.

'David ... don't,' she whispered later. They were still lying in each others arms but he had moved slightly.

'Don't what?' he queried and began to stroke her hair.

'Don't let me go ... just yet. I,' she turned her face into his shoulder, 'couldn't stand it ...'

He held her hard against him then and she began to shake from sheer reaction and he kept on holding her until she was still at last and able to look at him with tears in her eyes but a peaceful serenity too.

And her lips parted and she started to say something but seemed to change her mind and in the end it was only, 'Thank-you,' that she murmured.

He smiled. 'No. Thank-you, Lin. You're very special you know ...'

No I'm not, she thought dreamily, you are ... and fell asleep.

The only thing that pierced the radiant sort of daze she found herself in the next morning, was the remembered fact that she'd been going to say to him, I love you and only at the last moment had changed it to thank-you ...

She thought of it as she picked up the vanilla

dress. What would have happened if I had said it? she wondered as she smoothed the cotton folds of the dress and hung it up.

She stood staring at it in the cupboard with her hand still on the skirt. I feel like shouting it from the rooftops, she thought. I feel as if one day I won't be able to stop myself from saying it to him. But will he want to hear it? Will he feel he can't return it? Will he believe it . . .

A slight sound behind her brought her out of her reverie and she shook herself and turned to see David watching her.

'What is it?' he said with a slight frown in his eyes.

'Nothing . . .'

'Come here, Lin.'

She went to him a little uncertainly.

'Prove it,' he said and put his arms around her.

Her lips trembled into a smile. 'How?'

'Kiss me . . .'

She did, so warmly that the uncomfortable moment was lost and she forgot all about it and just about everything else until a knock on the door reclaimed them both to the fact that breakfast had arrived.

'What a pity,' David drawled, lifting his head at last. 'Shall I send it away?'

'Oh no!' she said laughingly. 'Is this going to become a habit? Making me miss my meals? Because if it is I might have to think about going on strike . . .'

'Might you now,' he murmured with the most wicked glint in his blue eyes and slid his hands beneath her wrapper to lie on her breasts.

'David!' she protested, still laughing, 'that's not fair!'

'All's fair in . . .'

'No it's not,' she interjected with a grin. 'It's just a saying people use to sooth their consciences. Besides, looking at it another way, you wouldn't want me to fade away from lack of proper nourishment, would you?' Her eyes danced impishly.

'Now that,' he said, withdrawing his hands and closing her wrapper up to her throat, 'makes sense. Why didn't you say so before?' He moved to the door and flung it open. 'Enter, my man!' he invited the patient waiter. This lady is in imminent danger of fading away from hunger! I was afraid she was going to start eating the flowers,' he said confidingly.

'Well, sir,' the waiter replied with a slightly wary look at Lineesa who was laughing helplessly, 'you did order breakfast for eight o'clock and it's exactly that. Or rather it was,' he amended, 'when I first knocked on the door, at least. But if,' he glanced at Lineesa again, 'if the lady has any special preferences, I mean if that's the problem, I'll do my best, sir, to procure them. My wife,' he added mysteriously, 'took to chocolate chip ice-cream topped with strawberry jam, for breakfast, for dinner, in the middle of the night! But it doesn't last for long,' he said consolingly.

'Serves you right,' Lineesa said, still giggling when the waiter had departed after David had stared at him uncomprehendingly for a few moments and then had found himself explaining a little ruefully that that was *not* the problem.

'You could have helped me out,' he said darkly. 'I had no idea what he was talking about at first. I thought he was a little touched in the head.'

'And *he* thinks I am—thanks to you!'

'You started it all, though,' he accused.

'All I wanted was my breakfast,' she said

innocently. 'In order to keep my strength up,' she added demurely.

'I'll remind you of that a bit later,' he said broodingly.

And he did. And said afterwards, 'I'm converted ... From now on we'll breakfast royally *every* day ...'

CHAPTER SEVEN

THREE days later they landed at Mascot Airport in Sydney and were walking through the terminal hand in hand, when he looked at her ruefully and said, 'Mrs Livingstone might not be best pleased with me.'

'Oh? Why?'

He stopped walking and swung her round to face him. 'Because,' he said, his eyes roaming over her in a way that was becoming familiar, 'you look lovelier than ever, but a little tired.'

'I shouldn't,' she said with a smile growing at the back of her eyes. 'I've spent a lot of time lately, flat on my back.'

He took a sudden breath and said, 'I wish I had you flat on your back right now.'

A faint tinge of colour stained her cheeks but she glanced around wryly and looked up at him again, in mock alarm, and he laughed a little. 'It's all right, I'm not as far gone as that. I'll be content with the thought. And this.' He bent his head and kissed her gently on the lips.

A discreet cough disturbed them and David released her leisurely and turned round and through their still linked hands she felt him tense slightly.

But he said in perfectly normal tones to the tall man in a sober grey suit who looked to be about David's age and was standing behind them, 'Harvey! This is a surprise. Where's Mike? Has anything come up?'

'Several things, David, old man, and I have a

letter for you from Mike. How do you do, Mrs Marchmont,' he added, but he'd had his dark eyes on Lineesa all the time. 'I don't believe we've met.' He took his eyes off her and cocked an eyebrow at David.

'Lin, this is Harvey Whiteman,' David said with an odd undercurrent of impatience in his voice. 'He's the Managing-Director of Marchmont Enterprises.'

'How do you do?' Lineesa murmured and they shook hands.

'David obviously doesn't believe in mixing business with pleasure, Mrs Marchmont,' Harvey Whiteman said holding on to Lineesa's hand for a fraction longer than necessary, and smiling whimsically. 'We—that is, those of us employed by him, had quite given up hope of ever seeing you in the flesh ... apart from Mike Smith, that is, the lucky dog! So this is a very great pleasure and may I say that your pictures don't do you justice, lovely as they are ...'

'You appear to be doing justice to a major speech, Harvey,' David said irritably.

'Not at all,' the other man replied imperturbably and winked boyishly at Lin. 'You look well after your little holiday, David,' he said, turning back to his employer. 'Which is a good thing,' he added significantly, 'because in your absence the Adelaide deal has come to the boil and we're now getting down to brass tacks, I think, but need your eagle eye and ruthless bargaining technique to bring it to a successful conclusion.'

David swore beneath his breath, then said abruptly, 'All right, Mike can brief me on it ... what did you say about a letter from Mike? I was expecting him to drive us home.'

'I arranged with Mr Livingstone to do that. He's

waiting in the car park. I have the letter here.' He handed David a long white envelope which David tore open. His eyes narrowed as they scanned the contents of the letter he extracted and Lineesa held her breath for some inexplicable reason as a premonition seized her. Had Mike resigned because of what had happened that night?

But she was destined to remain in ignorance for some time because David folded it again and said briefly, 'I see. Then you'd better come home with us, Harvey. Mr Livingstone can drive you back later.'

'I'm sorry,' David said later that night.

Lineesa was getting ready for bed and since they'd arrived back at Marchmont, David had been closeted with Harvey Whiteman apart from a short break when they'd joined her for dinner.

'It seems an age since I've dined at Marchmont,' Harvey had said, pointedly or innocently Lineesa was not quite sure but she'd felt suddenly awkward and she'd avoided looking at David, as she'd wondered how many people had suddenly found themselves cut off from Marchmont over the past year on account of her . . .

'You don't have to be sorry,' she said quietly in reply to David. 'Business is business.'

He watched her for a while in silence. She was brushing her hair and she had on a white nightgown with a dull-gold stiffened silk robe over it that was belted at the waist.

Then he said. 'I'm afraid that's true. What's more I shall be flying to Adelaide tomorrow for a few days.' He paused as she stopped brushing and their eyes met. 'You'll,' he smiled slightly, 'be able to have a rest.'

She began to brush her hair again but more slowly. 'I . . . don't need a rest,' she said softly. 'I could come too. I've never seen Adelaide for one thing.' She smiled at him impishly.

For a moment it seemed as if he was considering it. But in the end he said rather flatly, 'No. I have meetings scheduled almost non-stop. It would be pointless.'

She said nothing.

'Lin?'

She took a breath. 'All right. But I'll miss you. Is ... something wrong?' She looked at him questioningly.

'Why do you say that?' He returned her look piercingly.

Why do I? she asked herself. It's as if ... our aura has changed, become strained in some way, from—almost from the moment we landed. Or am I imagining it?

'I don't really know.' She shrugged her gold clad shoulders and put her brush down on the bureau.

'Yes, something is wrong,' he said then with an underlying note in his voice that she couldn't decipher.

Her eyes flew to his face and she felt her heart beginning to beat swiftly in fright at what he might say.

'I've just discovered,' he murmured a little indistinctly as he reached for her and drew her into his arms, 'how much I'd dearly love to be living on an uninhabited desert island with you where no business could intrude.'

The last bit was said into her hair and when she tilted her head back to look up at him in a sudden rush of relief that left her feeling weak at the knees, he started to kiss her throat.

'Oh David,' she whispered, 'this might have to be our desert island then, right here ...'

He didn't agree or disagree, simply picked her

up in his arms and laid her on the bed in the apricot bedroom which she'd come to think of as a prison but now promised to be a haven of delight, and as he started making love to her, she had no inkling how prophetic her words were to be ...

He was in Adelaide for nearly a week—a week that Lineesa took slowly despite her protestations about not being tired. She went to see her mother several times, however, and found her looking well.

'It's this new doctor I'm under, my dear,' her mother had confided. 'He's got me on a different set of pills and I feel like a spring chicken!'

'All the same, Mum, I was wondering whether you shouldn't have a ... sort of live-in companion.' She looked around the lovingly furnished lounge and hid an inward grimace as she spoke. For someone as particular as her mother, it could be a nightmare trying to find a suitable companion.

And indeed her mother protested vigorously for a moment or two, then fell strangely silent.

'What is it?' Lineesa queried and blinked to see her mother blush faintly.

'As a matter of fact I've ... made a rather special friend, Lineesa,' she said awkwardly.

'Well then ...'

'I mean a gentleman friend,' her mother interposed. 'Does that shock you? You must know your father meant more than anything in the world to me, apart from yourself, and that I will always honour and cherish his dear memory but ... it's been so long,' she said a little wistfully and added, 'I suppose you think it's very silly for someone my age to ... well to be even thinking about it.'

'Darling,' Lineesa said when she'd recovered her breath, 'no I don't! Please tell me about him.'

Her mother looked at her intently and brightened perceptibly. 'He's my new doctor. He's a few years older than I am but he's English too and we seem to ... have a rapport, you see. He lost his wife some time ago. He ... I ... there is a problem though,' she went on seemingly unaware that Lineesa was recovering from her second shock in about two minutes. 'He's a partner in a large suburban practice but he's been thinking for some time of scaling down his activities and ... well,' she took a gulp, 'he's been offered a partnership in a much smaller, less busy practice, a semi-country practice which would mean moving ... to the country, semi-country that is.'

Lineesa said, as her mother watched her anxiously having delivered herself supremely uncomfortably of her last few sentences, 'I don't see the problem. Don't you want to move? I would have thought the country, semi or otherwise would appeal to you.'

'It does,' her mother said miserably. 'But after all your hard work which paid for this lovely little house, I'd feel terrible leaving it. I'd feel as if I'd betrayed you somehow. I don't think I could do it!'

Lineesa sprang up and crossed to her mother's chair, 'Dearest mum,' she said, kneeling down beside the chair, 'you had me worried! I thought there was some real problem. Now you listen to me,' she said sternly but taking her mother's hands into her own, 'the only thing that would betray me, would be for you to pass up an opportunity for love and companionship which you've gone without for so long, on account of a house! So just ... discard that problem because it isn't one. When do I get to meet this gentleman?' she added softly.

It had been arranged for the next day and Lineesa too had fallen under the spell of the tall, silvery-haired man who had so captivated her mother.

'And a doctor too!' she said to Mrs Livingstone later that day. 'She couldn't have chosen better.'

'What's he like?' Mrs Livingstone was mending linen in the sewing room.

'Very correct, very distinguished looking and very sweet. They both are. They were holding hands when I left.'

Mrs Livingstone smiled. 'Love's a strange thing, Mrs Marchmont.' She glanced at Lineesa and her face softened further and she thought, I'll never understand what was between you and Mister David, but if I'm any judge, it's worked itself out, thank heavens. Because I never thought he'd ever let someone get real close to him after what happened . . .

'. . . Mrs Livingstone?'

Mrs Livingstone came out of her reverie with a start and a little shiver which she couldn't quite suppress. 'What was that?'

'Nothing really,' Lineesa said with a grin. 'You were just looking at me a bit strangely.'

'You're a sight for sore eyes, Mrs Marchmont,' Mrs Livingstone said. 'Especially since you came back from your holiday,' she added.

Lineesa blushed much as her mother had done the day before and thought later, well of course Mrs Livingstone has to know . . . certain things. She couldn't possibly tell from just looking at my face.

Yet when she drove over to see Bronwen the following day, who was now only weeks away from the birth of her baby, it seemed she *could* read Lineesa's face.

'Why, Lin,' she said placidly, 'it's good to see
...' She stopped and her blue eyes sharpened. 'It's
very good to see you,' she amended. 'Particularly
looking so well and happy,' she added significantly.

Lineesa said wryly, 'Not you too. I must have
looked a picture of misery before ...' She too
stopped speaking abruptly and bit her lip. She and
Bronwen had never discussed anything of a
personal nature, which had suited Lineesa admir-
ably although she'd often wondered, from
Bronwen's point of view, whether it was because it
was simply not her nature to speculate on other
people's affairs, even her own brother's, or
whether she was being supremely tactful—or, if
she'd been warned off by David.

But now there was something so direct in
Bronwen's eyes as she studied her sister-in-law,
Lineesa found herself unable to look away from it
and heard herself saying at last, 'I am ... happy,
Bronwen. Happier than I've ever been.' She
hesitated. 'That must sound strange to you
but ...'

'No,' Bronwen said a shade dryly. 'Sit down,
Lin. I've just made this tea, would you like a cup.
Um ... move all that laundry aside,' she pointed
to a chair with an over-flowing linen basket on it
and reached for another cup. 'No,' she said again,
sitting down carefully herself. 'I always knew
David would make some woman's life hell,' she
said quietly. 'And the minute I laid eyes on you, I
realised it was going to be you.'

'But ... then you must have known about me
and Piers after all,' Lineesa said uncertainly.

Bronwen shrugged. 'Yes I did.' She smiled. 'It
was hard not to. He was so full of you. But that's
not what I meant.'

'I don't understand . . .'

'It all goes back to our stepmother, Lin. She was a lot younger than our father. And she was absolutely gorgeous, and a little bit like you to look at.'

Lineesa's lips parted and her eyes were stunned.

'At least,' Bronwen went on, 'on first impressions. When I got to know you, I realised it was only the most superficial likeness, the same coloured hair basically,' she said ruefully. 'But she was also elegant and . . . well, to get the point, she took my father for the all time ride. She only married him for his money and his position, she cheated on him, she made his life a misery, she made our lives miserable but,' Bronwen smiled sadly, 'he never got over his infatuation for her and that was the saddest thing of all. To see him utterly dependent on her every whim . . .' She looked across the room unseeingly for a moment then went on, 'David—took it hardest.'

'He . . .' Lineesa's voice was a little hoarse, 'he said Piers took it hardest.'

'Piers was affected too, of course. We all were. But Piers was a lot younger and never as close to Daddy as David was.'

'And,' Lineesa said shakily, 'that's why he was totally sceptical about me?'

'Not just you, all women,' Bronwen said wisely. 'But perhaps you particularly because you had the same kind of magnetism . . . a slight resemblance, and because you'd attracted Piers undoubtedly, and you attracted him.'

'I . . .'

But Bronwen went on. 'I once thought,' she said meditatively, 'that if David ever found a woman he was afraid he would love and not be able to leave, he'd *make* himself do just that. I'm glad I was wrong.' She glinted a smile at Lineesa and confessed wryly, 'I didn't know how to take you at first, you know. David—was like a pillar to both of us, Piers and me. He still is to me in some ways. But now, I'm sorry if I wasn't much help to you. I wanted to be, Lin, after the first few months but I didn't know how and anyway, to interfere in other people's lives is to invite worse havoc,' she said intensely. 'And,' she reached across the intervening space to touch Lineesa's hand, 'in the end, you've wrought the miracle yourself. At least, to be looking so radiantly lovely, I think you must have.'

Lineesa blinked away some tears and put her other hand over Bronwen's. 'I ... he,' she said tremulously, 'I—I once tried to write a poem about it. When I first saw him it was like running into a brick wall in the dark. Then I thought I hated him as I hadn't believed it was possible to hate anyone. But all the time I wanted to *prove* myself to him somehow. It ... seemed to matter even when I couldn't understand why. It was always there at the back of my mind although I couldn't admit it. And you see, because of Piers, I felt so guilty ...'

'Lin,' Bronwen said gently, 'I think we all feel guilty about Piers in a way. I know I do. I feel there must have been something I could have done to make him understand that speed *kills* but none of us ...' She shrugged.

'But if I hadn't ...'

'No, Lin,' Bronwen interrupted. 'That's not valid and that's what I'm trying to say because it could just as easily have been a moment of great *elation* that prompted him to put his foot down flat to the board. But *none* of us can be held responsible for that patch of oil on the road. That's what he never understood.'

'You're very kind,' Lineesa said tremulously some moments later.

'That's not being kind, just honest.'

'All the same, most devoted sisters probably wouldn't have seen it that way.'

'Oh, I think they would have. But anyway, let's put it all behind us now. Isn't this bliss?' she said with a sigh. 'Such perfect peace and quiet!'

Lineesa looked round ruefully. 'Where is everyone?'

'Simon's taken the kids out. I threatened to lie down and expire if he didn't give me a couple of hours break,' she said darkly. 'Some days I feel as I've been pregnant all my life!'

When David got back from Adelaide, their reunion was passionate and loving, so much so that Lineesa said eventually and with a teasing little smile, 'Now I know why you didn't want to take me with you!'

'Oh?'

They were lying side by side in a pool of golden light on the wide bed in the apricot bedroom.

'Yes. We'd have missed this.'

He traced the outline of her naked body from her breasts to her thighs. 'Then,' he murmured, 'are you saying I should do it more often? Leave you behind I mean.'

'It has its compensations.'

He raised his head on one elbow and suddenly there was something almost sombre in his eyes as he said, 'Lin, you'd have been bored and I would have been . . .' He hesitated.

'Distracted?' she whispered with her lips twitching, and an imp of mischief dancing in her eyes.

'Yes . . .' he said, but there was no answering smile in his eyes.

She stared up at him and then sat up feeling suddenly cold and reached for the sheet. 'I was only teasing you. I . . . whatever you feel is best is fine for me.'

'Then lie down again,' he said after a moment and slid his hand round her back and under the sheet to touch her breast.

She shivered slightly. 'David . . .' Her voice cracked.

'Lie down, Lin,' he said quietly and plucked at her nipple gently.

She caught her breath but some instinct, an instinct for self-preservation she realised, a long time afterwards, seemed to be telling her to take a stand but about what, she didn't really know. And in a surge of confusion mingled with the undeniable clamouring of pulses his touch on her was arousing, she lay back but tensely.

'This is what I feel is best for—us,' he said and began to kiss her body in a way that was no match for her, that rendered her quivering with desire and when she moaned distractedly in her throat, he slid his leg between her thighs, and she was lost—quite lost to the beauty of his lovemaking even although it was such a short time since he'd made love to her before.

And she fell asleep in his arms afterwards.

But the next morning she remembered that curious instinct and the sombreness she'd seen in his eyes, and found herself trying to analyse it with a strange feeling of fear in her heart. But in the end she decided that she was worrying about nothing. It was natural that things couldn't be quite the same as they had at Shute Harbour. And it would be unreasonable to expect him to take her on every business trip. But I didn't expect it really, she thought. And I *was* only teasing last night . . .

oh hell, she mused, forget about it, you're imagining things . . .

Yet it seemed as if she couldn't quite persuade herself of this although she pushed it as deep into her subconscious as she could.

But two months later, her worst fears were realised and she was no longer grappling with some will o' the wisp she didn't quite understand because she was beginning to understand some things only too well and so painfully that no amount of wrestling with her subconscious would allow her to pretend otherwise.

And the basis of it was, that outside the four walls of the apricot bedroom at Marchmont, she and David were progressively drifting further and further apart, and seemingly at his instigation. What had begun at Shute Harbour and promised so much, had never eventuated. Their lives had become a series of passionate lovemakings and not much else. Even their social obligations had been pruned back, deliberately she suspected, and had to be thankful although hurt all the same, because to be in company with David had become like crossing a minefield blindfolded. If any man complimented her, she saw the ever more familiar look of acute impatience in his eyes that she'd seen for the first time when they'd landed at Mascot and Harvey Whiteman had been there to meet them. But it had got worse. It had become tinged with distaste and for hours, sometimes days afterwards, he would be moody and tense. And she, correspondingly, tense and uncertain and sometimes stiff with nerves.

But what can I do? she asked herself once. It's not as if I ever go looking for it. Perhaps I should wear Purdah . . .

Then one autumn morning when she was alone at Marchmont, as she had been for most of the month, she leant her head against the bedroom window-pane and gazed out at the choppy waters of the river, and thought, I *am* in Purdah ... That's what's happened. This is the desert island he spoke of but while he can come and go, I have to stay under lock and key. How strange—I might as well only be his mistress, someone he desires and supports but keeps out of the way of the rest of his life. I've exchanged one kind of prison for another ...

Tears fell on to her hands and suddenly she was crying desperately and found it hard to stop. But finally she washed her face and sank into one of the sherbet-green armchairs with her head laid back wearily.

'The thing is,' she murmured out aloud, '*why*? Was Bronwen right? Is that what's happening? Or is it much more simple—that he's never *loved* me, he only wanted to make amends and I subconsciously wished it into more? But even the way we were before we got home ... why did that change so *soon*?' she whispered painfully.

And even if it is Bronwen's fear come true, that he's deliberately building this wall between us, what can I do? Tell him how much I love him? I never have because ... because I was afraid to. Afraid to hear what he would say in return ... But if I tried to explain it to him, and at the same time tell him that however many men look at me, I could never even think of them ... should I do that?

She took a deep breath and stared abstractedly into space. It couldn't be worse than this ... half-life, she thought with sudden determination then. I feel as if I'm dying slowly ...

And didn't know how wrong she was.

But it was over a week before the opportunity presented and then, the way it happened was hardly auspicious, to put it mildly. In fact the reverse. It all came out in a stormy confrontation that had unbelievable consequences.

He came home from yet another business trip looking tired and strained. All the same he took her in his arms and kissed her lingeringly. Then they sat down to the dinner Mrs Livingstone had prepared and later, took their coffee into the lounge. Mr Livingstone had built a log fire in the huge grate and it was burning cheerfully and casting flickering shadows on the panelled walls.

'Tell me about your trip,' she said as she curled her legs beneath her on the settee.

He was sprawled out in an armchair opposite and for a few minutes he didn't answer, then he moved his shoulders and said idly, 'There's nothing much to tell. Unless you're interested in a bitter battle with the Painters and Dockers union. Let's see, Cathy Corbett was on the plane this afternoon, that's about the only thing of interest. By the way, I'll have to fly back to Melbourne tomorrow afternoon.'

Lineesa said, as a stab of sheer torture struck her heart, 'Will Cathy Corbett be on that plane, too?'

'What the hell do you mean by that?' he said after a moment.

She took a breath and cursed herself. Why did Cathy Corbett—even just the mention of that name, inevitably seem to plunge her into unwary statements and worse?

'I . . .' She bit her lip and decided the only thing she could do was make a clean breast of it. 'Someone told me, last year, that you and Cathy were seeing a lot of each other. At the time it didn't seem to be any of my business but . . .' She tailed off helplessly.

'Now it is your business, you think?' he queried coldly. 'Is it also going to be your business to imagine I'm sleeping with every woman whose name I mention, Lin?'

'David, no, of course not,' she said with difficulty. 'I . . . look, there's something about Cathy Corbett that rubs me up the wrong way and in fact it's not so surprising. She herself . . .' She stopped.

'What?' he shot at her through gritted teeth.

Lineesa sighed. 'Told me once . . . well, confirmed in a way what someone else had told me.' She shrugged and looked down at her hands.

'I have never,' David said with a steely precision, 'slept with Cathy Corbett. But our families have been friends ever since I can remember, and yes I was quite frequently in her company last year, but not in that way. She . . . was very fond of Piers. You shouldn't pay too much attention to malicious gossip, Lin.' He shot her a contemptuous look. 'Nor should you wilfully misinterpret what people say to you.'

Lineesa raised her head and a glint of anger lit her hazel eyes. 'I'm sorry, from your point of view,' she said very quietly. 'But at the same time I can't help knowing that Cathy would prefer it to be . . . more, than a family friendship. Nor was she too particular . . .' she hesitated, 'I mean . . .'

He waited, his eyes narrowed and piercing.

'Well, it occurred to me,' Lineesa said honestly, 'that she wasn't too particular about which one of you she got. She tried to warn me off Piers too.'

There was silence and it seemed to stretch interminably. Until he said drily, 'Thus the minds of women work.'

Lineesa closed her eyes and thought, no, don't say it, count to ten, do something! but don't say it. Yet she did.

'Does your mind work so differently, David?' she asked. 'Isn't that what you suspect of me every time I'm let loose in company? That I'm devious and conniving or if not that, that I have to be locked away in case I succumb to any man who happens to look at me, as if I was mindless and thoughtless and *stupid*? And isn't that what you think of me when you shut me out of your life and won't talk to me about anything that matters, or *anything*? When you use me for one thing only? Sex,' she said bitterly and wiped away a tear. 'You told me it would be different. You were wrong.'

'You should have told me you objected to that, although I don't see much evidence of it in bed,' he said coolly.

She took a shaken breath and scrubbed at her face. 'I ... that's not what I meant. I don't object to it. But I want to be your wife in every way, not just in bed. I love you, David. I think I always did.' She lifted her eyes to his. 'Did you never stop to wonder why I was so vulnerable to the things you did to me and ... always will be? I could never have been so easy to hurt for a ... just a physical attraction. Is ...' her voice sank to a whisper, 'is that all it is for you? I've hoped and prayed not but if it is, I'd rather you told me ...'

He looked away at last and his voice was barely audible as he said, 'I'm sorry, Lin ...'

She started to shake uncontrollably.

'But you're wrong about one thing,' he said. 'What you might think is love now, only looks that way to you because this is the first time it's happened for you. It's really ... the kind of thing

Mike Smith went through. Intense, painful but it will pass.'

Her lips parted.

'Mike left me because of you,' he said. 'He did the honourable thing. In that letter, he said he could no longer remain in my employ while he cherished the feelings for you that he did, and he added, meticulously, that you had in no way encouraged him. Which I believe. But the point is, do *you* believe Mike will spend the rest of his life in love with you?'

'I . . . David, it's not the same,' she whispered desperately.

He smiled tiredly. 'Lin, if there's one thing I want for you, it's for you to be happy. I . . . can't do that for you, and you've told me tonight just how well I'm succeeding at doing the opposite. So I think now, the time has come to really . . . call it quits. And then, one day you'll find a man that you can bestow your beauty and your warmth and your *true* love on, and if you think of me at all, I hope it will be only to remember that of all the things I did to you, I did at least one constructive thing—I taught you not to be afraid of sex, I . . . released the warmth and the generosity that you'd barricaded within yourself . . .'

No, no . . . oh God, no! something seemed to be screaming inside her head so that she didn't hear his last words. What have I done? What have I *done*?

Then she realised he'd stopped speaking and the only sound was the crackling of the logs in the grate because even the voice inside her head stopped, and she realised he was watching her and that his eyes were filled with compassion.

'I . . .' She licked her lips. 'I'd rather you'd left me the way I was if this is the way it's going to be,' she said huskily. 'I'd rather I didn't know what it's like to make love, than have to forget . . . the way you do it to me. *Please*,' she whispered but when he didn't say anything and she saw hazily, through her tears, the frown that came to his eyes and the way his lips set, she knew she was beaten, and she turned away and bit her lip until she drew blood and battled for some kind of control.

But it was several long minutes before she turned back to him and managed to say, 'I'll go . . . tomorrow. Will you—arrange everything?'

'Yes. But you don't have to go tomorrow. You don't have anywhere . . .'

'Yes I do. My mother's house is empty but of course,' she stopped self-consciously, 'I mean . . .'

'It's your house, Lin,' he said. 'I transferred the title deeds into your name some time ago. Also, you won't have any financial problems, I'll arrange that. What will you do?'

'Get a job. I don't know. David, I don't want to take any money from you, other than to tide me over . . .'

'No, Lin, I *owe* it to you . . .'

'But . . .'

'No buts, my dear,' he said quietly. 'How do you think your mother will take it?'

'She . . . I . . . if I tell her it's what I want to do, she'll understand. And now that she's got someone herself . . .' She shrugged. And thought, that's strange, isn't it? Life's funny.

'Why don't you go away for a holiday?' he said gently.

She didn't answer.

'Lin,' he sat forward, 'if ever you need anything, don't hesitate to come to me.'

She stared at him. And what if I find I need you to love me, that I can't live without you? she thought. What would you do then? Because that's the only thing I'll ever need from you . . .

'All right,' she said with an effort. 'Thank-you.'

He stood up and reached down to take her hand in his and pull her gently to her feet. 'Goodbye, my dear,' he said very softly and kissed her hand.

Her eyes flew to his.

'I think it's best if I go back to town tonight,' he said evenly. 'I'm *sorry*, for everything. But one day you'll understand that you're better off without me.'

'David . . .' Her cheeks were wet again and her eyes imploring but he only stared down at her with a frown of pain in his eyes and then bent his head to touch his lips briefly to hers. Then he released her hand and walked out of the room without a backward glance.

And a few minutes later she heard his car drive away and it was as if she was in the grip of a nightmare that was all too real.

Only . . . not even an hour, she thought dazedly as she stared around the room, it took me less than an hour to accomplish this. And why? Because I wanted more than he could give but now I've got *nothing* . . . just nothing. Oh God! What a fool I was. I could have put up with anything rather than this . . .

She sank down on to the settee and buried her head in her hands and wept.

And finally fell asleep on the settee where Mrs Livingstone discovered her the next morning.

'I don't believe it!' Mrs Livingstone said with tears in her eyes. But in the end she had to.

'You mustn't blame Mister David,' Lineesa said when Mrs Livingstone had made it abundantly plain that she simply didn't believe Lineesa's tentative explanation that it was a mutual decision to part.

'Oh, I know who to blame,' she said viciously and slammed a jade green powder bowl on to the vanity unit. They were in the bathroom where she'd chivvied Lineesa into having a warm bath in case she'd taken a chill from sleeping uncovered on the settee all night. '*Her*. The one who fouled *everything* up. The one who used to preen and primp herself in this very bathroom and got in all this ... green muck because it matched her eyes. She had eyes like a cat, you know, the last Mrs Marchmont. She *was* like a cat, a sly, diabolically clever she-cat. That's who to blame! If you knew ...'

'Mrs Livingstone it's not ... please,' Lineesa said whitely.

'It should have been changed, all this,' Mrs Livingstone went on though, with a wide sweep of her arm. 'But he wouldn't let me. It was as if he wanted to keep it all the same, like a warning to him. Oh no, Mrs Marchmont,' she said to Lineesa, 'don't try and tell me you want to leave him. I know better! There,' she said in suddenly softer tones, 'don't cry, child. I wish I could help. But all I can say is that I thought you were right for him, so right, and that I grew to love you nearly like a daughter ...'

CHAPTER EIGHT

LINEESA stuck her key into the front door and shivered. It was dark already and cold. Winter's closing in, she thought, and frowned and began to fumble as she heard the 'phone inside start to ring.

'Coming,' she muttered and pushed the door open and tripped, dropped one of the packets she was carrying which happened to contain her dinner, and snatched the receiver up convinced it would stop ringing at the same time.

But Ben Mason, with whom she'd worked for the past nine months, was nothing if not persistent, and he said into her ear before she got a chance to speak, 'My dear Lineesa, did I get you out of the bath?'

'Oh, it's you, Ben. No, but you made me drop my Chinese dinner and I suspect it's now leaking on to the carpet. Can you hang on a minute.'

She dealt with the carton of Sweet and Sour Pork which had indeed begun to leak and picked up the 'phone again, impatiently. 'What is it?'

'You sound cross.'

'I'm not cross.'

'Good, then you'll come out to dinner with me,' he said authoritatively. 'I've just had a brainwave about a series of interviews for you to do.'

'Ben . . . I'm tired,' she said and pulled the mail she'd taken from her post box out of her coat pocket. 'Could it wait for tomorrow? I . . .' She stopped speaking with her fingers resting on one long, rather bulky envelope that bore a familiar logo of the legal firm of Saunders & Saunders and her hand tightened briefly on the 'phone and she said a little breathlessly, 'All right. Thank you I'd like to. Where and when?'

She put the 'phone down a few minutes later and stared at the envelope for a long time before opening it with her mother's paper-knife and hands that weren't quite steady. But the contents contained no surprises and she folded the document up again and slipped it into the drawer of the telephone table.

She turned away and stood with her head bowed for a few minutes. Then she walked down the passage into her bedroom.

'You look lovely, as usual, my dear,' Ben said and ushered her into a secluded, comfortable banquet in the dimly lit restaurant. 'I think we'll have our aperitif right here at the table so we won't be disturbed. Is that dress new?'

Lineesa looked down at the simple topaz woollen dress she wore as if she'd never seen it before. Then she said with an effort, 'No . . .'

He didn't say anymore until their drinks arrived. Then he watched her sip hers for a few moments and said abruptly, 'Tell me what's wrong. No,' he held up a hand, 'don't try to deny it. I know you too well now.'

'Ben . . .' She stopped and looked at him. He was in his late-forties and his voice was known to most people in Sydney because he hosted a morning radio programme that contained a variety of segments, a talk-back session, live on-air interviews among them, and once a week an in-depth recorded interview with an interesting or famous person with Lineesa doing the interviewing.

She travelled far and wide to record these

interviews and loved the job, and the inner
confidence she gained as she realised she had a
flair for getting people to talk naturally and
unreservedly.

And she still had to pinch herself sometimes,
figuratively, when she thought back to how she'd
got the job. Ben Mason had read some of her
published verse and contacted her via her
publisher to arrange an interview with her. She'd
been reluctant but he'd been persistent and
persuasive and finally she'd agreed.

Yet no-one had been more surprised than she
had, after the interview had gone to air, when the
producer of the programme had offered her the
special interviewing job on a trial basis.

'You have an excellent voice for radio,' he'd
said. 'And the kind of poise that's needed. And
you'll have an assistant to help you with the
research . . .'

To Lineesa, at the time, anything to take her out
of herself had been like manna from heaven, and
she'd accepted despite her nervous certainty that
she'd done nothing to deserve this unexpected
bonanza, which had provided too, gradually,
several friendships among the people at the sation,
particularly with Ben who never pried or probed
into her past life, and whose sometimes malicious
wit was bracing and stimulating.

'Ben,' she said again, 'I don't really want to . . .'
She stopped and sighed. 'I . . . as of today, I'm
free. I'm no longer Mrs David Marchmont except
in name, if I care to use it I suppose, but then I
haven't for the last—over twelve months so I'm
not likely to start now. The final divorce papers
came today.'

'Do you want to tell me about it?' he said after a
moment. 'Sometimes it helps. But I won't press you.'

'I . . .' she hesitated and fiddled with her coaster, then found herself talking, telling him what she'd never imagined she'd tell anyone, telling him it all.

'And that's . . . what happened,' she said at last. 'Funnily enough my mother wasn't really surprised. She said she'd suspected that something was wrong. I always underestimated my mother, you know,' she added with a little frown.

'Don't we all,' he murmured.

'His sister still writes to me. And Mrs Livingstone sends me fruit cakes and last month, a knitted scarf. And the lawyer who handled the divorce forwarded a letter to me from the Muller's, it was their baby . . .' he nodded and she went on, 'which thanked me for all I'd done and said that they'd had her baptised Rosemary Lineesa . . . I think David might have suggested Rosemary because I used to call her Rosebud . . . Oh God,' she said with her hand to her mouth and tears in her eyes.

'And you've never seen him or heard from him again?' Ben said.

'No.'

'My dear,' he said after a long silence, 'I know how you feel. I . . . my wife died five years ago. She—we didn't meet until we were both well past out salad days. And then we only had two short years together. I couldn't believe, when she died, that fate could be so cruel. That it could finally find me someone to love in more ways than I'd dreamt possible, and then take her away from me. I ranted and railed and tried to tell myself I'd be better off if I'd never laid eyes on her, than have to endure the anguish of losing her. But I was wrong.'

'I've tried to tell myself the same thing,' Lineesa said thickly. She took a shuddering breath. 'I've

told myself all the old platitudes, that I'll grow
from this and be a more mature, wiser person
because of it, that to love and to lose is better than
never to have loved at all. But all the time I have
this terrible fear ... If I could be sure that he
didn't love me, I *should* be, because he never told
me any different, but if I could be absolutely sure,
I ... I'd hate the thought of that too, but I might
one day be able to live with it. But if it was as
Bronwen said, then I feel I failed him. I should
have been content to let ... perhaps time would
have healed him, if I'd been patient. But at other
times, I've thought it was only ever what I wanted
to believe, and I've hated him again a little and
hated myself a lot, and been impatient with myself
... and cursed myself for being a fool.'

'Lin, it's nothing so complex. You *can't* answer
for him, only for yourself. You can't say I should
have done this or that because you did more, and
endured far more than most people would have.
All you can say, is that you loved him, and maybe
always will ... don't thrash about like this, my
dear. Accept that, and one day it will bring you a
kind of peace, believe me ...'

She didn't believe him but she thought about what
he'd said often over the next weeks.

She was still living in what she always thought
of as her mother's house, surrounded by many of
her mother's knick-knacks. It seemed that the
gentle doctor she'd married had too been a great
collector of knick-knacks and some pruning had
had to take place to fit both their possessions into
their rustic retreat in the Blue Mountains. Once a
month Lineesa spent the weekend with them, and
if there was anything that had provided her with
some consolation since leaving Marchmont apart

from her job, it had been to see how happy her mother was.

For the most part though, her lifestyle had revolved around her mother's house, the beach where she walked for hours in all kinds of weather, and where she swam when it was warm enough, and the little garden her mother had so loved and cherished. After neglecting it at first, it had claimed her and she'd discovered she'd inherited her mother's green fingers so that it had blazed with colour during the long, hot summer.

All of this, her domesticity and care of the house and garden had endeared her to her mother's friends and neighbours, who apparently decided that she couldn't be so bad after all, despite her altered status and gradually she found she was on nodding terms with a host of middle-aged men and ladies who populated the suburb.

And it was one Sunday when she was planting seedlings that would bloom in spring, that she found herself thinking yet again of Ben's words. It was about six weeks after the final divorce papers had come. And suddenly, with half a box of seedlings still to plant, she got up and went inside and washed her hands. Then she went into the lounge and studied the bookcase thoughtfully and finally found what she was looking for—a slim volume of Australian poetry. She held the book by its spine and shook it gently until a piece of paper fluttered out. She picked it up and carried it to the small writing bureau and stared at it for a long time. Then she reached for a pen and began to write. What she wrote didn't take very long and her lips moved silently as she read it over once . . .

How can you explain a hatred that isn't always that

*How can you put it into words that don't sound
trite
How can you put it into words at all
When it's like some dark, hidden depth to your
soul?*

*Then there's love—sometimes that says hate too
It says all right, if I'm not good enough for you
I'll climb on my horse be it ever so flimsy
And pretend I was never, never possessed by this
whimsy.*

*But now I can say I loved you this day
Though I don't know why it happened this way
But I can't regret it nor ever forget it . . .
I loved you is all I can say.*

She closed her eyes and when she opened them
they held a shimmer of tears but a kind of
tranquillity too. And she picked up the piece of
paper and tore it into shreds and let them flutter
into the waste-paper basket and reached for the
'phone.

'Ben?' she said into it a few moments later. 'It's
Lin. I thought of having a few people around
tonight for an impromptu dinner party. Is it too
short notice for you? . . . Oh Good! About
seven . . .'

She made three more 'phone calls and her
invitation was accepted each time with varying
degrees of surprise because it was the first time
she'd invited anyone home.

'That makes two, four—six of us,' she murmured
and sprang up. 'I better get cracking or
impromptu will be only too true . . .'

The months slid by. But these months were
different. She not only entertained at home in a

small way but accepted a variety of invitations to go out, and she thought she was content with her busy working life and burgeoning social life and the only time a flicker of doubt crept into her mind, was when some man began to take more than a social interest in her. She found it impossible to respond and was always on the look out for it so she could 'nip it in the bud' as Ben, who sometimes saw a great deal too much for comfort, remarked to her once.

'But even that will come one day, my dear,' he'd gone on to say gently. 'As it is, you've made great strides . . .'

Then one day when there was more than a hint of spring in the air, she accepted an invitation to go to the races with the technical-director of the programme and his wife, both keen race-goers who'd been pressing her for some time to go with them. They owned an eighth-share in a thorough-bred three-year old which was to have its first start from a spell that afternoon, and should win—according to Murray and Pat, that was. However, they expected him to win every time he set foot on a track and the fact that he let them down more often than not, didn't ever seriously dent their enthusiasm although their pockets were another matter.

In fact it was something of joke at the station and Lineesa was thinking about it and smiling a little wryly to herself as she donned her new spring outfit, a soft green linen dress with a pleated skirt and a cravat neck and a lightly padded, quilted silk jacket with a cream background and little flowers in an identical green as the dress. She wore elegant taupé suede court shoes and had a matching slim, suede clutch purse. She thought of putting up her hair but in the end, left it loose to lie in a curling, dark-gold cloud on her shoulders. Pat would be wearing a hat, she knew, for Pat was very modish but as she didn't have one to match her outfit, she decided not to bother.

But as she arrived at Royal Randwick—she'd arranged to meet them on the course—she suffered a slight pang. It was not the course that Piers had taken her to but she'd never since been able to set foot on a race-course without recalling the day he'd introduced her to everyone as a cousin of the Queen.

I've managed not to think of Piers for a long time now, she thought and bit her lip. Then she deliberately closed her mind to the past, and walked across the grass to meet her friends.

'What did I tell you?' Murray cried after the sixth race and kissed his wife first and then Lineesa. 'Two lengths he won by and at twenty-five-to-one! That's incredible!'

'Too right, mate,' a disgruntled looking man standing beside then said, 'and I'll tell you bloody why! The favourite was crook and the kid on the second favourite shouldn't be allowed to ride rocking horses. Didn't you see how he nearly brought the whole field down? That's why your twenty-five-to-one shot got up when it should by rights have run twenty-five lengths last!'

'My dear sir!' Murray said, drawing himself to his full height which wasn't very tall, 'You're talking to a part owner, I'll have you know ...'

'It'd have to be,' the man replied with a dour shrug. 'Horses aren't the only ones to wear blinkers, y'know.' And he walked away.

'What a thoroughly nasty person!' Murray said crossly but Pat and Lineesa were convulsed with laughter until Pat said, 'There, there, dear, let's go and lead him in—we're the only members of the syndicate here today.'

Lineesa, who had a guest ticket to the owners stand, was not allowed into the enclosure but she stood at the fence and watched her friends with a warm look in her eyes.

Then she turned and glanced idly across another fence that enclosed even more hallowed ground, that set aside for committee members of the Australian Jockey Club and their guests, and her eyes widened as they came to rest on a tall figure in a beautifully tailored light-grey suit with his back partly turned to her.

It couldn't be . . . it is, she thought incoherently and her purse slid out of her suddenly nerveless fingers.

She bent down to retrieve it with her heart hammering uncomfortably and when she straightened, David had turned fully towards her, only a few feet away from her across the fence and his eyes were resting on her indifferently and with no recognition in them, as if he was scanning the crowd for want of something better to do, and she held her breath and wanted to run but wanted to stay, in fact was rooted to the spot anyway, in a sort of breathless paralysis as she waited for his eyes to pass on . . .

But they didn't. They narrowed instead and then widened in recognition and his lips parted in surprise and the hand he held his race-book in, clenched suddenly round it.

And Lineesa found herself doing the strangest thing. She smiled, a radiant, beautiful smile that made him catch his breath although she didn't know it. All she knew was that just to see him again filled her with an incredible feeling of warmth and a kind of joy. It's been so long, she thought, it seems like a lifetime, a dry thirsty lifetime but just to be able to look at him like this . . . is to be restored . . .

Then he moved sharply, and the moment was broken. Her smile died as he looked around impatiently as if for a gate and she took fright— and flight. She turned away and a flood of noisy punters engulfed her and she allowed herself to be borne along with the tide and as far away as possible from the committee enclosure.

In fact she did more than that. She found Murray and Pat at the stables, made an excuse to them that she had a headache, and left.

She drove home slowly and feeling curiously at peace. Ben was right, she mused. You can come to terms with it and I think I've finally proved to myself today, that I have . . . He looked—tired but otherwise just the same. Did he want to speak to me? Perhaps, but only on the spur of the moment because he's always known where to . . . find me. And I didn't want that, just to see him was enough . . .

Her state of peaceful euphoria lasted all the way home. Then, with a suddenness that took her breath away, it deserted her just as she was fitting her key into the door. It literally seemed to seep away like rainwater into parched, drought-stricken earth and she found she was shaking so much the key wouldn't go into the lock and she stared at the front door and didn't see it but instead, a vision of what the rest of her life was going to be—like a never-ending tunnel of loneliness and grief and a yearning to be loved by and be able to love just one man . . .

She dropped the key and reeled against the verandah wall and covered her face with her hands, and knew that she'd deceived herself and never more so than this afternoon because she hadn't come to terms with the fact that she'd loved and lost David Marchmont, she never would . . .

She didn't hear the car pull into the driveway as she leant against the wall and wept into her hands more bitterly than she'd ever done in her life.

Nor did she see the tall figure in a light-grey suit emerge from it and mount the front steps slowly.

In fact the first intimation she had that she was not alone, came only when she heard her name said . . .

'Lin . . . *don't*,' David Marchmont said, and took her in his arms.

'David . . .?' She lifted her flushed, tear-streaked face incredulously, and tensed convulsively.

He didn't answer, just looked down at her with his blue eyes sombre and filled with pain until her tears welled again and she tried to turn her head away.

But he wouldn't let her. He pressed her head into his shoulder and she was so stunned, she didn't resist, just clung to him helplessly, unbelievingly—hopelessly.

And she didn't remember much about how he got her inside, just that he did and that he laid her down on the settee, took her shoes off and put one of her mother's hand-embroidered cushions behind her head. Then he disappeared down the passage and reappeared some minutes later with a half-full bottle of sherry and two glasses.

'That's terrible sherry,' she said huskily. 'Someone brought it . . . I've had it for months.'

'No matter,' he said and smiled slightly. 'It's all there is.' He poured it carefully and handed her a glass.

She sipped the harsh, golden liquid and took a shuddering breath. But it seemed to have a steadying effect. 'I'm all right really,' she said with a sketchy attempt at a smile. 'I don't know what got into me. Did you ... I mean, why did you come?'

He sat down and studied the glass in his hands for a moment, then his lashes lifted suddenly and their gazes locked, 'To talk to you—find out how you are. It's been ... a long time.'

She swallowed and sat up and drank some more sherry. 'I'm fine,' she said again, looking away. 'I've made a new life for myself and it's not one I'm ashamed of. It's creative in a sense and ... fulfilling. I'm content.'

'Are you ... happy?' There was a faint undertone of harshness in his voice.

She looked at him briefly and winced inwardly because his eyes were probing hers with a piercing directness. And to gain time and composure, she drained her sherry glass and set it down precisely in the middle of a crocheted doily on the small table beside the settee.

'I told you, I'm content,' she said quietly. 'Happiness comes and goes. No-one can be happy all the time. But I feel as I've achieved something and that's worth a great deal to me. Are you ...' she looked at him, 'content? You said once that you wished that for me. I ...' she hesitated, 'would very much wish that for you too,' she finished barely audibly and looked down at her hands.

'Lin,' he said abruptly, 'can I tell you something I've never told anyone else?'

'If ... if you want to,' she said with a tiny frown knotting her brow. 'About ...?' She tailed off uncertainly.

'About me. It happened to me when I was very young. That's the only thing I can say in my defence, that I was very young—not much older in fact, than you were when I first met you. I ... fell in love with an older woman, at least that's what I thought it was. It would be more accurate to say I was besotted.' His lips twisted grimly. 'And nothing I told myself, none of the good sense and wisdom I tried to offer myself, stopped me from having an affair with her, although she was married. Not even, for a time, the incredible deceits we had to indulge in.'

He stopped speaking and looked past her and there was something so terrible in his eyes, she caught her breath and felt her heart contract with an awful sense of premonition.

'And they were incredible, those deceits,' he said at last and brought his eyes back to her face. 'They have to be, you see, when you're having an affair with your father's wife—your stepmother.'

She closed her eyes.

'Exactly,' he said grimly.

Her eyes flew open. 'David . . . no, I didn't mean that,' she whispered.

He smiled but without humour. 'All the same . . . but let me tell you all of it. She was very beautiful. She was about twenty-nine when this . . . started. And my father was in his late forties. I was about twenty-one. And the insane thing was, I'd always resented her and never particularly liked her. Yet the day came when I *fell* for her, even although I knew she was . . . inviting me to, and what kind of a person it made her. It was like being drunk, high . . . I don't know.' His voice changed. 'But in the end, the deceits we practised were superfluous, other than that they at least prevented Bronwen and Piers from knowing the whole truth. Because when my father accused her one day of having a lover, she didn't deny it. In fact she told him who it was. He didn't believe her—he didn't want to believe her. But there *was* one other person who knew about it. And she told him to ask Mrs Livingstone if he didn't believe her . . .'

Lineesa licked her dry lips. 'I'm so sorry,' she whispered. 'I didn't know.'

'Apart from Mrs Livingstone, who only found out accidentally in the first place, no-one knows now although I've sometimes wondered if Bronwen *did* suspect after all.'

'I think she might have,' Lineesa said slowly. 'She told me once you . . . that . . . well, also that I reminded her a little of your stepmother.'

'I thought that too—but only briefly. It was an illusion.'

'But it didn't help either,' she said with a frown of pain.

'No.' He was silent, then he looked at her questioningly. 'You said also—what else did Bronwen tell you?'

She looked away. 'David,' she said with difficulty, 'why have you told me this?'

'Because I wanted you to understand why I had to send you away, Lin.'

'But why now? If you couldn't tell me then, why now?' she said hoarsely and confusedly. 'And I don't really understand. Were you *so* sure I was or would become that kind of woman?'

'No, Lin. Oh, I sometimes told myself all women were the same basically. I told myself all the old clichés . . . You see, what happened was that I fell deeply and helplessly in love with you, oh yes,' he said and their eyes caught and held again, hers sparkling with new tears and his suddenly weary beyond words. 'I began to know that as soon as we got home from Shute Harbour. The symptoms were classic, jealousy, not wanting to be away from you . . .' He shrugged.

'David,' she whispered but he interrupted her.

'While I thought it was only an intense attraction mingled with respect and affection we— *I* felt safe, Lin. But once I admitted to myself it was more than that, in fact the very thing I'd sworn never to let happen to me, it seemed as if I had to tear it apart. I... it was as if I was at war with myself all the time. I tried to tell myself that there'd only ever been the most superficial resemblance between you and her, that you weren't and never could be the kind of woman she was. But at other times, when I saw men looking at you the way they'd looked at her, I thought of my father and, I realise now, I used that to fuel the normal kind of jealousy most men in love with a beautiful woman feel, into something more. I ... it was as if something inside me just couldn't accept that I *loved* you because I couldn't conquer the fear that I'd live to regret it one day.'

'I ...' She tried to speak but found she couldn't.

'So you were right and you were wrong that last night, Lin,' he said. 'I was trying to set you apart from me, but not for the reason you thought. I was trying to keep you—but *prove* that I could keep you at a distance. But that night too, some sanity prevailed. I could see how hurt you were. And I knew I couldn't go on hurting you like that. So I did what I thought was best for us.'

Lineesa's tears fell on her hands. She tilted her head back but they trickled down her throat and wet the cravat tie of her dress as she cried silently.

Then she managed to take hold of herself and she wiped her nose on the back of her hand and said, 'That's what Bronwen told me. That,' her voice shook, 'if you ever found someone you loved and thought you'd not be able to leave, you'd make yourself do it. She told me a bit about your father but not ... only that it had affected you most. I didn't know what to think . . . I mean,' her voice sank, 'deep down I thought that you couldn't have loved me as I . . . thought I loved you.'

Something flickered in his eyes, something she couldn't decipher as she stared at him helplessly. Then he said, 'I can't ask you to forgive me but perhaps if you could understand a little.'

'I do,' she whispered.

His eyes searched her face. 'Lin,' he said at last, 'this afternoon when I saw you again and you smiled at me I thought—I didn't know what to think. Then something like panic came into your eyes and you slipped away before I could talk to you and I knew I had to. That's why I came here, hoping you'd be here. You were, but . . .'

She moved her hands to cut off his words, 'David,' she said uncertainly, 'I don't . . . I . . . women are emotional creatures. They cry a lot and for no real reason.'

'You were crying as if,' he said with an effort, 'your heart was broken, Lin.'

She closed her eyes.

'Lin?' he said gently.

She took a breath. 'I . . .' she whispered but she couldn't go on.

He said finally, 'Seeing those two things, you smiling and then crying, gave me a spark of hope, Lin.'

'H-hope?' the word seemed to stick in her throat.

'Yes . . . I have no right to tell you this after what I did to you, Lin,' he said huskily, 'but when I saw that beautiful, shining smile I . . . these last so many months have been like a slow form of torture to me. Because the only thing I proved to myself as time went by, was that while I might be able to get you out of my life, I couldn't get you out of my heart. I thought of you in so many ways. If the weather was cold I wondered if you were warm enough. Whenever I saw Bronwen's new baby, I thought of you with another baby and how you were at Cooper Creek. Whenever I saw a group of kids, I wondered what our children would have been like. I sat down to a meal of grilled, freshly caught fish once and all I could think it was you, fishing off the jetty at Shute Harbour with no real intention of ever catching a fish ...' He smiled painfully. 'I made some excuse and got up and left. Those were the kind of thoughts that constantly caught me unawares—so many of them and such little things. But there were others, the things I thought about when I was alone—some other man making love to you, you carrying someone else's child, you ... frightened of the way men looked at you, and that I, knowing it, had let you go thinking I too had only wanted one thing from you.'

'David ... you could have ... oh, don't do this to me!' she cried, her breath coming in great gasps. 'You could have come to me—any time. But you didn't ...'

'I nearly came, so many times,' he said sombrely.

She put her hands up to her face. 'I wish you hadn't told me this,' she said despairingly, 'if ... because ...'

'I didn't come, Lin,' his voice was curiously unsteady, 'because like a rider to everyone of those thoughts there were others—always, and always the same. I thought, how could she possibly forgive me? I thought, she *must* hate me now and even that's more than I deserve after everything I've done to her. And I knew I couldn't bear to see that. The other thing was,' he said, 'there was no way I could prove to you that I no longer cared or resented how completely you possessed my heart. I could only say the words—that I'd finally come to understand that the wall of intolerable cynicism I'd built up in my heart, had only really been a cover-up for my own sense of guilt over what happened so long ago. I just ... couldn't see how you could believe that.'

Lineesa's hands sank slowly into her lap and it was her turn to stare at him searchingly.

'Then I thought today,' he said and his face was pale and drawn but his eyes were steady, too steady, as if they were preparing themselves for a blow, 'I thought, you wouldn't have smiled at me that way if you'd hated me, and you wouldn't have been crying like that if ...' He stopped and a muscle beat suddenly in his jaw.

'David ...'

'But if ... Lin, if it was only because you're a generous, sometimes sentimental person, if you're happy and you've put it all behind you, I'll go now ...'

'David, oh God,' she said hoarsely, 'if you only knew ...'

'You said, just now you said you thought I couldn't have loved you as you *thought* you'd loved me ... I'd understand ...'

'No you don't,' she whispered. 'David, will you do something for me? Will you take me in your arms and hold me?'

'Lin ...'

'Because without you I'm not happy and I'm not even content. I tried to pretend to myself that I was, and I tried to pretend to you that I was because I thought that's what you wanted to hear. Then I thought you were going to tell me that even although you loved me, there was no hope for us ever, so I said that . . . I don't really know why—I just couldn't bear to believe it. But the truth is, I'm barely alive without you, David. I hurt all the time and *nothing* I do stops it. So please,' she whispered.

She didn't remember how she came to be in his arms then, just that she was and that the small table and her sherry glass got knocked over in the process but neither of them noticed that at the time as he held her hard against him and kissed her tears and murmured her name over and over again until she stopped shaking and looked up at him with an unmistakable and radiant look of love in her eyes.

Nor did she remember much about him picking her up and carrying her to the nearest bedroom and undressing her with unsteady hands, although she knew she'd never forget their mutual hunger for each other that led him to take her without his usual finesse and as if he could never get enough of her, as if he'd truly been starved of her unbearably.

'I'm sorry,' he said afterwards with his arms still around her slender, naked body as if he'd never let her go. 'I've dreamt of doing this so often, dreamt of doing it just the way you like it most, slowly and . . . but instead I was like an impatient clumsy schoolboy. Did I hurt you?'

Lineesa gently cradled his fair head to her breasts and thought that she might die of sheer happiness. Because his urgent, driving need for her, his very lack of control that was so unlike him, had proved more to her, than he could ever know.

'No, my darling,' she said very softly and pressed her fingers through his hair. 'Because the way I like it, is any way you care to do it.'

He lifted his head. 'I don't deserve this,' he said huskily and kissed her lips gently, 'but will you marry me again, Lin?'

'If you promise never to divorce me again, David,' she whispered with a smile curving her lips.

'Oh Lin, what can I say...'

'Kiss me instead ...'

Coming Next Month

Available in May wherever paperback books are sold, or through Harlequin Reader Service.

In the U.S.
P.O. Box 1397
Buffalo, N.Y.
14240-1397

In Canada
P.O. Box 2800, Postal Station A
5170 Yonge Street
Willowdale, Ontario M2N 6J3

No one Can Resist . . .

HARLEQUIN REGENCY ROMANCES

Regency romances take you back to a time when men fought for their ladies' honor and passions—a time when heroines had to choose between love and duty . . . with love always the winner!

Enjoy these three authentic novels of love and romance set in one of the most colorful periods of England's history.

Lady Alicia's Secret by Rachel Cosgrove Payes

She had to keep her true identity hidden—at least until she was convinced of his love!

Deception So Agreeable by Mary Butler

She reacted with outrage to his false proposal of marriage, then nearly regretted her decision.

The Country Gentleman by Dinah Dean

She refused to believe the rumors about him— certainly until they could be confirmed or denied!

Everyone Loves...

HARLEQUIN GOTHIC ROMANCES

A young woman lured to an isolated estate far from help and civilization . . . a man, lonely, tortured by a centuries' old commitment . . . and a sinister force threatening them both and their newfound love . . .

Read these three superb novels of romance and suspense . . . as timeless as love and as filled with the unexpected as tomorrow!

Return To Shadow Creek by Helen B. Hicks

She returned to the place of her birth—only to discover a sinister plot lurking in wait for her. . . .

Shadows Over Briarcliff by Marilyn Ross

Her visit vividly brought back the unhappy past—and with it an unknown evil presence. . . .

The Blue House by Dolores Holliday

She had no control over the evil forces that were driving her to the brink of madness. . . .

What the press says about Harlequin romance fiction...

"When it comes to romantic novels...
Harlequin is the indisputable king."
   —*New York Times*

"...always with an upbeat, happy ending."
   —*San Francisco Chronicle*

"Women have come to trust these
stories about contemporary people,
set in exciting foreign places."
   —*Best Sellers*, New York

"The most popular reading matter of
American women today."
   —*Detroit News*

"...a work of art."
   —*Globe & Mail*, Toronto

Take 4 novels and a surprise gift FREE